**Kate Hardy** lives on the outskirts of Norwich with her husband, two small children, two lazy spaniels—and too many books to count! She wrote her first book at age six when her parents gave her a typewriter for her birthday. She had the first of a series of sexy romances published at age 25, and swapped a job in marketing communications for freelance health journalism when her son was born so she could spend more time with him. She's wanted to write for Mills & Boon® since she was twelve—and when she was pregnant with her daughter, her husband pointed out that writing Medical Romances™ would be the perfect way to combine her interest in health issues with her love of good stories. It really is the best of both worlds—especially as she gets to meet a new gorgeous hero every time…

Kate is always delighted to hear from readers—do drop in to her website at www.katehardy.com

For my big sister, Jackie, with love.

# THE CONSULTANT'S CHRISTMAS PROPOSAL

BY
KATE HARDY

Harlequin
Mills & Boon

Medical

DID YOU PURCHASE THIS BOOK WITHOUT A COVER?
If you did, you should be aware it is **stolen property** as it was
reported 'unsold and destroyed' by a retailer.
Neither the author nor the publisher has received any payment
for this book.

First Published 2005
First Australian Paperback Edition 2005
ISBN 0 733 56553 0

THE CONSULTANT'S CHRISTMAS PROPOSAL © 2005 by Pamela Brooks
Philippine Copyright 2005
Australian Copyright 2005
New Zealand Copyright 2005
Except for use in any review, the reproduction or utilisation of this work in
whole or in part in any form by any electronic, mechanical or other means,
now known or hereafter invented, including xerography, photocopying and
recording, or in any information storage or retrieval system, is forbidden
without the permission of the publisher, Harlequin Mills & Boon, Locked Bag
7002, Chatswood D.C. N.S.W., Australia 2067.

All the characters in this book have no existence outside the imagination of
the author, and have no relation whatsoever to anyone bearing the same
name or names. They are not even distantly inspired by any individual
known or unknown to the author, and all the incidents are pure invention.

This book is sold subject to the condition that it shall not, by way of trade or
otherwise, be lent, resold, hired out or otherwise circulated without the prior
consent of the publisher in any form of binding or cover other than that in
which it is published and without a similar condition including this condition
being imposed on the subsequent purchaser.

All rights reserved including the right of reproduction in whole or in part in
any form. This edition is published by arrangement with Harlequin
Enterprises II B.V.

Published by
Harlequin Mills & Boon
3 Gibbes Street
CHATSWOOD NSW 2067
AUSTRALIA

HARLEQUIN MILLS & BOON MEDICAL and the Rose Device are
trademarks used under license and registered in Australia, New Zealand,
Philippines, United States Patent & Trademark Office and in other countries.

Printed and bound in Australia by
McPherson's Printing Group

# CHAPTER ONE

SASKIA groaned. 'Oh, no. Why does my mobile phone have to ring the very second that my fajitas are about to turn up?'

'You're not on call, are you?' Toby asked, pausing before he poured her a glass of wine.

'Of course not. I wouldn't have let you order the wine if I was.' She scowled and fished her phone out of her handbag, then frowned as she looked at the display. 'Lydia?' She hadn't expected her best friend to call tonight. Anticipation prickled down the back of her neck. Paul was in Canada on business. Was there something wrong with the children? She answered swiftly. 'Hi, Lyd. Everything OK?' She tried to ignore the sizzling dish placed before her by the waitress.

'Saskia, thank God you answered. It's Paul.'

Saskia's smile vanished as she heard the panic in Lydia's voice. 'What's happened?'

'The hospital called from Vancouver. He's got appendicitis. Saskia, supposing it bursts before they remove it?'

'Of course it won't. They'll keep him under obs before the operation.'

'He could end up with peritonitis. Or an abscess.'

'True, but unlikely.'

'The incision wound might get infected.'

Saskia's eyes crinkled at the corners. 'Lydia, will you stop panicking? That's the worst thing about being a qualified doctor. You know all about the worst-case scenarios.' Lydia was a GP, currently on maternity leave.

'Why did it have to happen while he was away on busi-

5

ness? I can't get there. He's ill and he needs me, and I'm thousands of miles away.'

'Lyd, stop panicking. If they've already called you, that means he's probably in the operating theatre right now—so you wouldn't be able to be with him right now anyway. It also means they've got to him in time, the appendix is probably in a kidney dish somewhere, and they're probably sewing him up even as we speak.'

Lydia dragged in a breath. 'Yeah. Sorry. I'm...' Her voice tailed off.

'Worried sick. Of course you are, Lyd. Anyone would be. But they'll ring you as soon as he's in Recovery and he's come round from the anaesthetic,' Saskia soothed. 'Look, do you want Toby and me to come over and sit with you while you're waiting to hear?'

'I'm just being wet,' Lydia said, sounding embarrassed.

'No. You're missing Paul, you never sleep well when he's away—and I bet the second you dropped off, last night, Madam woke you up because she's teething. So you're sleep-deprived and husband-deprived, not to mention probably hormonal.' Helena, Lydia's youngest child, was only five months old. 'And we're your best mates, so we'll forgive you.' She put her hand over the phone and looked at Toby. 'Did you follow all that?' she asked.

He nodded. 'I'll get the fajitas "to go". We'll warm them up again when we get to Lyd's.'

She nodded. 'I'll fill you in on the rest of it in the car.' She took her hand off the phone again. 'Lyd? We're on our way.'

Five minutes later, they were on their way from Sheffield to the little Derbyshire village where Lydia lived. Toby stole a glance at the woman sitting in the passenger seat, who was making a list on her electronic organiser. Typical Saskia. Practical, organised everything and everyone, moved at the speed of light... He hadn't been able to resist buying her a T-shirt for her birthday with 'Superwoman' emblazoned across it. In Latin. She'd loved it.

The problem was, he couldn't get a certain picture out of his mind. Dr Saskia Hayward, wearing nothing but that T-shirt. And peeling it off...for him.

He fought to control himself. That was the other problem. Saskia made his knees weak: curvy, dark-haired, with grey eyes that could skewer you or soothe you, depending on her mood, and a mouth that would give any red-blooded man palpitations. But she didn't feel the same way about him. As far as she was concerned, Toby Barker was the medical student she'd met thirteen years ago—a shy, nerdy, bespectacled boy who'd become one of her two best friends. And 'best friend' meant no touching. Well, not touching in the way *he* wanted to touch her. A casual arm around her shoulder, a hug or a kiss on the cheek was fine. Saskia was the tactile sort, so it was a kind of sweet torture. Enough to make him want more, yet not enough to satisfy.

As troubles always came in threes, that was the third thing. Saskia went through men at speed, too. They almost never lasted longer than two dates. And two dates wouldn't be enough for Toby. Particularly as they'd mean he would be out of her life for good afterwards. At least being her best friend meant that he got to spend time with her.

All the same, he kept wondering what it would be like to kiss her. Well, actually, he knew what it was like to kiss her. He'd done it at a Christmas party two years ago, under the mistletoe. It had blown his mind. But then he'd seen the shock and horror in her face, so he'd started slurring his words and pretending he was drunk.

On sparkling mineral water.

But she'd accepted it, particularly as the next day he'd claimed he had a mammoth hangover and asked her to promise him that he hadn't done anything really embarrassing or stupid at the party the previous night. To his relief, she hadn't mentioned the kiss. So he'd got away with it. Just.

Though the kiss still haunted him. The softness of her skin. The way she tasted. And, oh, the way her mouth had opened under his. It wasn't long until Christmas. The party season would start in a couple of weeks. All he had to do was make sure they went to one together, then manoeuvre her over to some mistletoe and—

'Tobe, are you listening?'

'No,' he admitted. Not that he was going to tell her what he'd been thinking about. That was definitely something he needed to keep under wraps.

'I said, Lyd's fretting because she wants to see Paul. Until she can see for herself that he's fine, she'll be impossible. But no way can she take the kids with her. Apart from the fact that it's a long-haul flight, you can't expect a baby and a three-year-old to hang around a hospital all day and give Daddy lots of peace and quiet while he recovers from abdominal surgery.'

'They probably haven't arranged a passport for Helena yet, anyway,' Toby said.

'You're right. I hadn't thought of that. She's going to be caught right in the middle—wanting to be with Paul, but not wanting to leave the kids.' Saskia sighed. 'If she does go, she'll need someone to hold the fort. Her parents are in New Zealand, visiting her sister—and Paul's parents won't be able to do it.' Paul's mother was in the early stages of Alzheimer's and they both knew it wasn't fair to expect Paul's father to look after his grandchildren *and* his wife. She drummed her fingers on her knees. 'Which leaves me.'

'Saskia, can I just remind you that you have a full-time job? You're a senior registrar—you've been acting consultant since Jim's been on sick leave, getting his hernia sorted. No way are you going to get a couple of weeks' leave at this kind of short notice.'

'I don't need to. I'll cope,' she said airily.

That was stating the obvious. Saskia never saw problems, only solutions. She was a born coper. Give her ten seconds, and she'd have the whole thing planned out.

Toby began counting in his head. He got to three before she announced, 'It's easy. I'll move into the cottage while Lyd's away. I can drop the kids off at nursery before work, and pick them up at the end of the day.'

'And when you're on a late shift? Nurseries are open until six p.m. at the latest,' he pointed out. 'Actually, they don't open until eight, so it doesn't fit with early shift either. And even if you did manage by some miracle to get the kids into the hospital crèche until Lyd's home again, it's not fair to add another layer of disruption to their lives.'

'I suppose so,' she admitted, clearly unwillingly.

'Look, Saskia, we all know you're Superwoman, but you really can't do your job, run Lyd's house, as well as your own, *and* take over as a mum of two, all on your own.' He waved her protest away. 'It's more than just being flung in at the deep end. If Lyd wants to go over to Paul and you take over the reins from her, you're going to need help— preferably from someone who doesn't work shifts, or at least someone who's on an early when you're on a late, so one of you can do the nursery run while the other's at work.'

'And your solution is?'

Typical Saskia. She expected people to follow her lead and come up with answers, not questions. Well, he was a match for her on that front. 'I'll help you.'

She frowned. 'What do you know about kids?'

He tapped his index finger thoughtfully on the steering-wheel. 'Hmm, let me see. I'm a paediatrician.' Not to mention that he'd been a qualified doctor for three years longer than Saskia had. 'Does that count?'

She snorted. 'Sarcasm is the lowest form of wit. And working in Paeds isn't the same as living with kids, is it?'

'Says the woman who works with foetuses and babies under a week old. I've got as much childcare experience as you have. I've babysat for Lyd.' He was the first choice if Paul was away and Saskia and Lydia wanted a girly night out. In fact, now he thought about it, he'd babysat the children more often than Saskia had.

She sighed. 'You're probably right.'

'No "probably" about it. I couldn't cope all on my own either. This needs teamwork.'

She chuckled, obviously picking up on the fact that he was deliberately imitating her management style. 'All right, all right. Thank you. I accept. But don't tell anyone we're living together, will you?'

Why? Had she met someone?

'Or it'll ruin my reputation,' she added.

It was only then that Toby realised he was holding his breath. He grinned—more from relief that she wasn't about to embark on another romantic disaster than in reaction to her teasing. 'Ha, more like it'll ruin mine. *You're* the one who has strings of men and never gives any of them a third date!'

'Yeah, and you're the one who doesn't date at all.'

'Too busy with me job, luv,' he fenced, in his best fake Yorkshire accent. Yet another lie. But how could he tell her the truth? There was only one woman he wanted. And he was waiting patiently until she realised that he was the one she'd been looking for all her life.

It was just taking a bit longer than he'd hoped.

'Thanks for coming.' Lydia's eyes were puffy and red. 'I know he's in the best place but...'

'But you want to be there with him,' Saskia said, hugging her. 'Of course you do.'

'And I can't go.' Lydia's face was anguished. 'I can't drag Helena and Billy halfway across the world in the middle of the night—or even tomorrow morning. It wouldn't be fair on them. And I can't leave them. Not my babies.'

'Superwoman here said you'd say that,' Toby said dryly. 'And she's got a plan.'

'Yep. You go to Paul: we'll look after the kids,' Saskia said.

'But…Saskia, I can't expect you to do that! You're both working full time. Even if the nursery can have the kids for the extra hours, it's— I can't ask you to do that.'

'We're offering,' Toby said.

Lydia explained what they'd discussed in the car. 'They'll be perfectly safe with us.'

'But I've never been away from Helena before. Not for a whole night, let alone however long I'll be in Vancouver! And I've only been away from Billy for a couple of nights.'

'On your anniversary, when Paul swept you away for a romantic weekend and I babysat,' Saskia reminded her. 'Lyd, you can't be in two places at once. If you stay here, you'll get yourself in a state about Paul. If you go to Vancouver, at least you know you don't have to worry about the kids because they'll be with us. Toby gets to play with a train set all evening, I get to sing nursery rhymes…' She spread her hands. 'So everyone's happy. Helena's too young to know what's going on, and Billy's going to get spoiled rotten. You can ring him every day so he gets to talk to you, I'll get him to draw pictures to send to you, and Toby and I will text you several times a day.'

Lydia bit her lip. 'Thanks. And I love you for offering. But I can't.' She raked a hand through her hair. 'It's six weeks till Christmas. I haven't even started my shopping or thought about writing cards or—'

'Easy. Write a list on the plane, then fax it to me when you get to Vancouver,' Saskia said. 'And, no, it's not going to be a hassle. I can get most of it through the Internet.' She grinned. 'And I love spending other people's money.'

'There's no point in arguing with her, Lyd. You know she's got an answer for everything,' Toby said, smiling to take the sting from his words.

'Are you sure?' Lydia asked.

'Sure,' Toby said. 'And you'll be back home in time to do the tree with Billy. Now, go and pack. Saskia'll book your ticket. Where's your passport?'

'Uh—I dunno, somewhere in the filing cabinet.'

'GPs. They're so hopeless with paperwork,' Saskia teased. To her relief, it made Lydia give her the glimmer of a smile.

'I don't know how to thank you both,' Lydia said.

'Chocolate,' Toby said in a stage whisper. 'Now go and pack.'


'I'm sorry I ruined your dinner out,' Lydia said when Saskia came up to tell her everything was booked.

'Hey, no worries. It's not as if it was a hot date. Only Toby.'

'*Only?* Saskia, this is our best friend you're dismissing.'

'I'm not dismissing him.' Saskia shook her head impatiently. 'You know I adore Tobe. But he's not my man.'

'Pity. You two would be good together.'

Saskia scoffed. 'Forget it, Lyd. I value him too much to ruin our friendship like that.'

'Maybe it wouldn't be ruining it,' Lydia suggested quietly.

'Yes, it would. Stop matchmaking. I'm not cut out for marriage, and you know it. Anyway, I'm busy with my career.' Just as her parents had been. Saskia knew she'd been an accident, and not a happy one at that. Yes, she'd had enough freedom as a teenager to make all her friends envious—but she'd also grown up realising that her parents should never have got married, let alone had children. She'd learned from their mistakes, and marriage was definitely not for her.

As for the children part... Two months ago, she'd discovered that was going to be out of the question, too. Not that she'd bothered Lydia or Toby with that choice piece of information yet. She was still thinking about it, mulling over her options. Besides, Lyd was busy with her family, and Toby—well, she needed to sort his life out before she sorted hers. Find him a woman who'd give him the love and cherishing he deserved, because he sure as hell wasn't going to find one for himself. Toby never dated. And considering he'd told her on her twenty-first birthday—when they'd both drunk far too much champagne—that he wanted to get married and have six kids, the big noisy family he hadn't had as a child...

Ah. She'd sort her friends' lives out. And then maybe her own might miraculously fall into place while she wasn't looking.

'Right. I'm taking notes.' She waved her electronic organiser at Lydia. 'Helena's routine I pretty much know anyway.' Saskia was a frequent enough visitor to the Osbourne household to know when the baby was fed and had naps. 'You've got baby food in the freezer?'

'Frozen in ice cubes. She's on two cubes of savoury followed by two sweet or fromage frais. They're all labelled, and she's had them all before so you don't have to worry about her having a bad reaction to new food. There are pots of fromage frais in the fridge.' Lydia grimaced as she shut her case. 'One thing, Billy's decided he's eating nothing but chicken nuggets.'

'Ha. Aunty Saskia will have him on fajitas with extra jalapeños by the time you get back.' Then Saskia saw her friend's expression. 'Joke, Lyd. Of course I wouldn't give him jalapeños! Fajitas might be a good idea, though. If he gets to choose his own veggies, shredded chicken and a tortilla wrap, and he makes it all himself, he's more likely to try it.' Then she frowned. 'What?'

'Listen to you. Talk about child psychology. You'd make a brilliant mother.'

'Godmother,' Saskia corrected firmly. 'I'm not cut out for motherhood.' Especially now. Though she'd find a better time to tell Lydia about that. 'Now, I've phoned the nursery manager and explained it's a crisis. They're fine about having Helena and Billy from eight until four, or whenever Toby or I can get there. Toby and I will synchronise shifts tomorrow, so one of us is on an early while the other's on a late and we can work around nursery times. You can ring your folks on the way to Manchester airport and let them know what's happening. I've got the hospital's number in Vancouver, so I can leave messages there. Have you spoken to Paul's parents?'

'I'll ring from Vancouver, when I've seen him and can reassure them.'

'Good idea.' Saskia hugged her. 'Right, you're all set. Give Paul my love. And don't worry about rushing back. I know he'll be able to leave hospital in a couple of days, but no way can he tackle a long-haul flight for at least two weeks after the operation.' Preferably six, to make sure there were no complications. Though she wasn't going to remind Lydia about that in case she panicked again. Lydia had a cool head where work was concerned, but tended to act like a headless chicken at home. And the idea of Paul having to miss their daughter's first Christmas because he was thousands of miles away would make her cry all the way to Vancouver. 'Toby and I will be fine.'

'Yeah. You're the best.' Lydia hugged her back. 'Thanks, Saskia.'

'That's what friends are for,' Saskia said lightly.

Lydia paused by Helena's cot. The baby was lying on her back with her hands up by her head. Lydia leaned over to kiss her. 'My baby. Saskia, I can't bear this.'

'I'll take a picture of her every day and send it to your phone,' Saskia promised.

Lydia breathed in the baby's scent. 'My baby,' she whispered again.

'Your baby will be absolutely fine, I promise you,' Saskia said. 'I hate to rush you, but you've got a plane to catch.'

'I know.' Lydia kissed Helena one more time. 'I have to kiss Billy goodbye.'

'Quickly. And I'm not being horrible—the more drawn-out it is, the worse you're going to feel,' Saskia advised.

Lydia stroked Billy's forehead. 'Sleep well, honey. And Mummy's going to be home very, very soon,' she whispered. 'I love you.'

'And he loves you, too, and he'll drive you mad with questions about the plane when you talk to him on the phone tomorrow,' Saskia said, and shepherded her friend downstairs. 'Now. Handbag?'

Lydia grabbed it from the coatstand. 'Check.'

'Money?'

'Check. I'll change some at the airport.'

'Passport, Toby's sorting. Book to read on the plane?'

'I'll get something at the airport.'

'Passport.' Toby came into the hall and handed it to her. 'Saskia, you need to have a word with our Lyd about filing things efficiently.'

Lydia hugged him. 'Thanks, Tobe. I owe you one.'

'Any time.' He ruffled her hair. 'Come on, let's go—or I'll end up having to break the speed limit to get you to the airport on time, and I want to keep my licence clean.'

'Yes.' Lydia's voice wobbled, and it was obvious that

she was only just holding the tears back. 'I can't bear leaving them.'

'It's going to be fine.' Toby kissed Saskia's cheek. 'I'll pick up some clean clothes from your place on the way back,' he said.

Saskia had given him a spare key years ago, just as she had the spare key to his house on her keyring. It meant if one of them was on holiday the other could water the plants and generally keep an eye on things. 'Try to pick something that matches,' she said.

He snorted. 'You always wear a black or navy suit and a cream shirt at work. What's to match?'

'Shoes. I can't wear a black suit with navy shoes, can I?'

He rolled his eyes. 'Women,' he said, then winked at her and escorted Lydia to his car.

Saskia checked on both children—who were sleeping soundly—then rejected the idea of reheating her fajitas. She ought to wait for Toby, even though she knew it'd be at least four hours before he came back from the airport and their respective houses. She made herself a cup of coffee, raided Lydia's biscuit tin, took a novel at random from the shelves on one side of the fireplace and curled up on the sofa.

What an evening.

She'd gone out for dinner with her best friend, expecting a chance to chatter and have a glass of wine and put her problems out of her mind. And now she was facing possibly a few weeks of being a stand-in mum.

*Wife* and mum, seeing that Toby had put himself in the role of stand-in dad.

She shook herself. No. Her relationships were a disaster area, and she wasn't going to mix up Toby in that. She sighed, wishing Lydia hadn't even suggested it. She didn't want to think about Toby in that sense. He was her best friend. Sure, he was good-looking—the blueprint of tall, dark and handsome, with slate-blue eyes and that vulnerable mouth. He was funny, he was clever—he'd made consultant last year at the age of thirty-three—and he was genuinely nice.

In fact, she couldn't work out why someone hadn't snapped him up years ago.

But he wasn't the one for her. Was he?

# CHAPTER TWO

It was nearly midnight before Toby came back. 'I stayed to see Lyd onto the plane,' he explained.

Only Toby would be that thoughtful. 'You must be shattered. And starving,' Saskia said.

'I'm past it now—I couldn't face the fajitas. I hope you didn't wait for me.'

She shrugged it off. 'I wasn't that hungry anyway. Hey, I'll make you a hot drink. If you have coffee now, you won't sleep—so would you rather have camomile tea or hot milk?'

'They're both vile,' Toby grumbled. 'Nah, I'll be fine, but thanks for the offer. What shift are you on tomorrow?'

'Early. You?'

'Early. But I'll fix it so I can go in an hour later than you. I'll drop the kids off, you pick them up.'

'Sure. I'll book a taxi to drop me at work, and I'll pick my car up later.' She smiled. 'I made up your bed in the spare room.'

'Cheers. I'm ready to drop.' He handed her a small, bright pink case. 'I'm glad nobody saw me with this. Pink luggage. Now, *that's* embarrassing.'

She grinned. 'Don't be such a baby.'

'I sorted out a couple of shirts, two suits and two pairs of shoes.'

And underwear, she hoped. The idea of Toby picking out her underwear... She shook herself. No, this was her best friend. Not her lover. Not the man she wanted to surprise her with a confection in silk and lace. Not the man she'd dress up for.

Though she was aware it sounded as if she was trying to protest a little too much.

'Thanks. See you in the morning, then. Um, do you want the shower first?'

'Ladies first,' he said gravely.

She laughed. 'You'll regret that when I've hogged the bathroom for an hour.'

Mmm, and he could think of exactly how she could spend that hour. In the shower. With him. He shook himself. Hell, he must be more tired than he'd thought. He usually managed to suppress his fantasies about his best friend.

Usually.

Then again, he didn't usually live with her. OK, so they weren't sharing a room. Weren't sharing a bed. Other than that, they were living together as stand-in parents. Arranging things around the kids, like any other couple with a family. They'd even be making Christmas decorations together with Billy this year…

He reined in his thoughts. If he didn't watch it, he'd do something stupid. Like kiss her. Or sweep her off her feet. And then he'd lose her for good. No, he'd stay with the softly-softly approach. It would work, in the end. He just knew it.

'See you in the morning,' he said, and headed for his room before he gave in to temptation.

By the time Toby had showered and changed next morning, Saskia had already fed the children, strapped the car seat into Toby's car, made a pot of coffee and found out from Vancouver that Paul's operation had been a success.

'You're seriously scary,' he said, accepting a cup of coffee gratefully. 'And I love you for it.'

'Good.' A horn beeped outside and she looked out of the living-room window. 'Yes, that's my taxi. I'd better go.' She kissed the children goodbye. 'Be good for Uncle Toby,' she told Billy. 'I'll see you both this afternoon. And I'll see *you*...' she waved at Toby '...some time at work, so we can synchronise our duty rosters. Lunch?'

'I'll ring you,' he promised.

'*Ciao.*' And she was gone.

Toby tried to stifle his disappointment. As if she'd been going to kiss him goodbye, as well as the children.

But it would have been nice.

Odd, odd, odd. Saskia was used to *not* sharing her breakfast table. No crumbs or cereal on the floor, no spilled milk all over the table, and she could do the crossword and listen to the news on the radio in peace without having to make conversation with anyone else.

But it had been...well, nice. Helping Billy to smear butter and Marmite on his toast, having Helena blowing raspberries at her, seeing the children's faces light up as soon as Toby had walked in. It had never been like that when she'd grown up. Just a succession of nannies and then her parents, who'd insisted on complete silence at the breakfast table while they'd read the newspaper or a case brief.

She shook herself as she realised that they were at the hospital and the cabbie was waiting for the fare. Now was not the time to start fantasising about having a family. She had a job to do.

She paid the cabbie, gave him an extra tip to make up for her dozy behaviour, took the stairs to the maternity unit and started her ward round. No complications on the ward, so she did a quick round of the delivery floor.

'Saskia, I'm glad you're here. I could do with a second opinion.'

Saskia went straight onto red alert. Georgina Wilson was their senior midwife, and her instincts were always spot on.'What's up?'

'Clare Fellowes. First baby, due eleven days ago. We induced her yesterday morning with prostaglandins—two lots—and she was only just three centimetres dilated at a quarter to one this morning.'

Usually induction meant a fast labour—this one was unusually slow.

'Larissa broke Clare's waters at six this morning. It doesn't seem to have speeded up her labour at all.'

'OP?' The best position in labour was when the baby faced the mother's back. In OP, or occipitoposterior presentation, the baby faced the mother's front, so the head didn't press down as efficiently on the cervix, the baby's head needed to rotate further and labour tended to take longer.

'Yes. No sign of meconium.' Meconium was the baby's first bowel movement, a thick, greenish-black substance made up of bile, mucus and intestinal cells. If the baby passed it into the amniotic fluid, it generally indicated that the foetus was in distress—and sometimes the baby could inhale it when he started to breathe, when it would block his airways.

'That's good. What's the baby's heart trace doing?'

'Slightly tachycardic, with late deceleration.'

This told Saskia that the baby's heart rate was faster than normal, then dropping after the peak of Clare's contractions—a sign that the baby wasn't getting enough oxygen. 'Have you taken a blood sample from the baby's scalp?'

'Just about to. I've put the mum on her left side and given her some oxygen.'

'Well done. Let's stop the oxytocin and do a blood sample.' Saskia frowned. 'If it's not good, we're looking at a section. Does it say anything in her birth plan?'

'The usual. She wants a normal birth with minimal pain relief, hubby to cut the umbilical cord, and she'd rather not have an episiotomy if she can help it.'

Saskia winced. 'Please, don't tell me she's been going through a labour this long on just gas and air or a TENS machine.'

Georgina shook her head. 'When it was obvious she was in for the long haul, we talked over the idea of an epidural.'

'I hope she went for it. Giving birth is a tough enough job—why add to it by struggling with pain when we can help?'

Georgina smiled. 'You're preaching to the converted.'

'Yeah, I know.' Saskia smiled back.

Saskia introduced herself to Clare and her partner, explained what she was about to do and that it wouldn't hurt the baby at all, and took the blood sample. To her dismay, the pH value was 7.21, lower than it should be. Saskia examined Clare and realised immediately that the labour simply wasn't progressing as it should have done.

'Clare, you've done really well to get this far,' she said gently. 'You've had a tough first labour and you've been really heroic about it. But your baby's starting to show signs of distress, and his blood's slightly acidic. I'd recommend that you have a Caesarean section.'

'But…we wanted a natural birth.' A tear trickled down Clare's face. 'A normal one.'

'Sometimes you need a bit of extra help. It's your choice, but your labour's very, very slow and you're tired. The longer it goes on, the more the baby's at risk of having problems. At the moment, I'm concerned he's not getting enough oxygen.'

Clare swallowed. 'Does it mean I'll have to have a general anaesthetic?'

'Not if you don't want to. You've already got an epidural, so we'll just top it up a bit for the operation. Your partner can still come in with you to hold your hand all the way.' She smiled at Clare's partner. 'And you can still cut the cord, if that's what you want to do.'

'And the baby's going to be all right?' he asked.

'If we deliver soon.'

Clare nodded. 'All right.'

'Thank you. I just need you to sign a consent form. And in about thirty minutes, you'll be holding your baby.' She smiled again, and signalled to Georgina that she wanted a word outside. 'I'll find an anaesthetist to top up the epidural for the section. Can you ring Paeds and ask them to send someone up, please?'

'Sure.'

Once the anaesthetist was arranged, Saskia had another chat with Clare, explained what would happen in Theatre and answered Clare's questions.

Just after she'd made the incision, a masked doctor in scrubs walked into Theatre. She recognised his outline immediately, and smiled to herself. The baby was going to be in good hands, then. Toby's hands.

She worked swiftly but, as she'd dreaded, the baby had passed meconium. Inhaled some, too, by the green staining around his nose.

'You have a lovely little boy,' she told Clare. 'The paediatrician's just going to check him over, and then you'll be able to have a cuddle.'

She concentrated on sewing up the wound she'd made, though every so often she glanced over towards Toby. He was good at his job—very good—but the more time passed, the more likely it was that the baby was in trouble.

Finally, to her relief, she heard what she'd been waiting for. A baby's cry.

'One perfect little boy.' Toby brought the wrapped baby over to Clare. 'He's lovely. Well done.'

'Is he all right?'

'He's going to be fine,' Toby reassured her. 'He did inhale a bit of meconium, but we've got rid of it and there won't be any long-term damage. Congratulations.'

'My little boy,' Clare said, and burst into tears.

'I love happy endings,' Toby said a couple of hours later, as he unwrapped his sandwich. 'I think we should have cases like that every day.'

'Meconium inhalation isn't my definition of a good day,' Saskia said dryly. 'How were the kids?'

'Fine. They had the play-dough out at nursery, so Billy couldn't wait to go and make something. You're still OK to pick them up?'

'Yep. Did you bring your diary?'

'You're such a slave-driver.' He pulled a face at her. 'How does your ward put up with you?'

'They've learned how to be efficient,' Saskia said sweetly.

He pulled his diary from his jacket pocket. 'OK. I've got two days I can't switch—meetings that can't be moved— but otherwise I can be flexible.'

Saskia took a quick look at his schedule and compared it with hers on her organiser. 'Actually, we won't have to do that much switching. Say it'll be two weeks until Lyd comes home. If you can change your late to an early on Friday, and I swap my Monday late for an early, we're about there.'

'Done. Now can I eat my sandwich in peace?'

'We haven't done the cooking rota yet. And, before you say it, no, we are *not* living on take-aways, Toby Barker.'

'How about whoever's home first cooks dinner, and who-ever's on a late has it heated up when they get in?' he suggested.

'Fine. I'll be home first tonight, so I'll cook.' She handed him a key. 'Here.'

'What's this?'

'My spare car key. We'll need to swap Billy's seat be-tween our cars, depending on who's doing the nursery run.'

Helena was still in an infant carrier, which made it easier to transport her.

'My spare car key's at home.' He sighed. 'And you don't have to nag me. I'll make a detour and pick it up after work. And I'll drop his car seat up to you before you go.'

'Attaboy.' Saskia took a sip of her coffee. 'Ah, bliss.'

Toby had other definitions of bliss that definitely didn't involve coffee. But he would have liked to put that expression on Saskia's face.

Maybe one day.

The rest of the day passed without incident. Toby remembered to collect his spare car key and some more clothes. But when he let himself into the house, he stopped dead. Saskia was sitting on the floor in the living room with Helena asleep on her lap, and Saskia and Billy were both waving chiffon scarves around. In the background, a CD of rippling piano music was playing. Billy's face was bright with excitement and he was chattering away, and Saskia was answering the little boy's questions, looking relaxed and happy. They looked like any mother and child, clearly adoring each other and enjoying some special time together until Daddy came home.

This was what his life could be like if...

Stop. Don't rush her, he warned himself. You know her background. She's pathologically scared of the marriage-and-family bit. Let her get used to this, then maybe, just maybe, she'll consider trying something like this permanently.

'Having fun?' he asked lightly as he walked into the living room.

'We're doing seaside music,' Billy told him. 'Look, Uncle Toby, we're making waves.' The little boy was waving the scarf up and down, in perfect time to the music.

'Very creative,' he said to Saskia. 'Maybe you should

switch specialty—we could do with someone like you in Paeds.'

An odd expression—one he couldn't read—flitted across her face. Then he wondered if he'd imagined it, because she smiled. 'I can't take the credit for this. Billy learned it at preschool music class—I've taken him a couple of times when I've been off duty.'

He hadn't known that. This really wasn't what he'd expected from Saskia, but he liked this side of her. The side she kept hidden. It made him wonder what else he had to discover about her after all these years.

'You can do music with us, Uncle Toby.' Billy rummaged in a bag and presented Toby with a white scarf.

'Sure.' He sat down and joined them. 'I like this music.' It wasn't Saskia's normal style. She normally listened to rock. Loud and fast. Just like Saskia herself.

'It's Ludovico Einaudi—*Le Onde*. "The Waves",' she explained. 'Think yourself lucky we're not doing Saint-Saëns' "The Aquarium" from the *Carnival of Animals*.'

'Aunty Saskia made us some special seaweed for music class, out of a dustbin bag. And shiny fishes,' Billy said. 'You have to hold the fish and dance to the music.'

Toby raised an eyebrow. 'You kept that quiet. What else are you hiding, Saskia?'

To his surprise, she blushed. 'Nothing. Hey, Billy, do you want to sing your new Christmas song to Uncle Toby?'

'Yeah!' Billy stood up and started to sing 'Christmas Shamrock' to the tune of 'Frère Jacques'.

'Shamrock?' Toby whispered in Saskia's ear. 'Since when has shamrock been Christmassy?'

'They're doing world cultures at nursery,' Saskia muttered back.

Billy finished up with a rendition of what he called the 'Sneezy Song'—'When Santa Got Stuck Up the Chimney'—with a little bit of prompting from Saskia when he forgot the words.

They both clapped him when the song ended, and he beamed. 'I can sing it to Mummy tonight.'

'You certainly can.' Saskia smiled at him, and turned briefly to Toby. 'It's my turn to cook tonight.' She hugged her godson. 'Billy, do you want to draw a picture for Mummy with Uncle Toby while I cook tea?'

'I'll get the felt pens!' the little boy said gleefully, and raced off to fetch them.

'I'm doing pasta,' she whispered to Toby, 'so I can disguise vegetables in the sauce. Tomorrow, it's your turn to come up with a clever strategy to get him to eat something other than chicken nuggets. I told Lyd we'd do the impossible.'

'You *would*,' Toby said, resigned. 'Right. I'm going to draw Billy a super rocket. And we're going to call it after you.'

'Oh, ha.' She grinned, and headed for the kitchen.

As soon as Saskia was out of Toby's view, she massaged her fingers and took some painkillers. Was this a flare-up? And would the flare-ups become more frequent as time went on? she wondered.

'Not going to happen. It's *not*.' If she could stop the disease in its course by sheer will-power, her hands would stop hurting right now.

She flexed her fingers. Unfortunately, will-power wasn't going to cure rheumatoid arthritis. And there wasn't much chance of getting a cure in her Christmas stocking either. Damn, damn, damn. She'd managed in Theatre earlier today without any problems. But, right at this moment, no way could she have held a scalpel. She couldn't have supervised a junior surgeon either—because if the younger doctor got into a mess, she wouldn't be able to step in and take over.

She was going to have to resign. And soon. For her patients' sake.

But medicine was her whole life. If she gave it up completely, what would she do? How would she fill the empty hours?

It took her ages to chop the vegetables for the pasta sauce. But she persisted—no way was she giving in. She wasn't *ready* to give in.

Just as the sauce started to bubble, Billy bounded into the kitchen and shoved a piece of cardboard into her hand. 'We made you a card,' he announced.

'"To the best aunty in the world. Love Billy,"' she read. There was a picture of a flower on the front, coloured in bright pink and purple, and Toby had drawn Billy's name in dots for the little boy to join up. Shocked by the tears that rose to her eyes, she blinked them back, hard. 'Thank you,' she said, crouching down to give Billy a hug.

The sauce was a success, too. She'd put it in a blender so there were no tell-tale lumps of vegetables. Billy ate his meal without a hint of protest, and scoffed more garlic bread than anyone else. He also managed to get garlic butter in his hair and spaghetti sauce over his face—even behind his ears.

'Bathtime?' Toby suggested.

'Yep. You're in charge tonight. I'm doing the washing-up.' She didn't want to share the chores with him in case he noticed just how long it was taking her to do things—and then asked awkward questions that she didn't want to answer.

'Both of them together?' he asked, looking nervous.

'C'mon, you're the paediatrician. And you must have bathed your godchildren at some point.'

'Nope. You and Lyd always do it.'

True. Saskia adored bathtime with the children, playing splashing games, then wrapping them in a towel 'like a sausage roll', as Billy called it. She loved Helena's gummy smiles of delight as she splashed, the clean, baby-soft scent of the children's skin after a bath, the way Billy's hair stuck up in tufts. She loved giving them their milk, a cuddle, a story, tucking them into bed and then reading another story, because she couldn't resist Billy's huge eyes and cute smile when he asked so nicely for just one more.

But tonight she physically couldn't do it.

'You'll enjoy it,' she said, forcing herself to sound happy and bubbly, the Saskia Hayward that everyone at the hospital knew. The super-focused doctor, who partied at night and burned the candle at both ends.

As Toby took the children upstairs, Saskia's smile faded. It wasn't going to be that way for much longer. In fact, it'd get to the point where she wasn't going to be burning candles at all.

Laboriously, she washed up. By the end, she knew that drying up would push her just that one step too far. The dishes could just air-dry tonight.

She couldn't resist going to see how Toby was getting on. To her amusement, he was on his knees next to the bathtub, holding Billy's plastic frog and joining in with Billy's version of 'Five little speckled frogs'. She couldn't help grinning at the gusto with which Toby sang 'Yum, yum' about the delicious flies the frogs were eating, and 'Glub, glub' as the frogs jumped into the pool.

Toby looked just like any other father enjoying bathtime with his kids while giving his wife a break from childcare.

This was what her life could have been like, if…

No ifs, no buts. She'd made her choice a long time ago. It was the right one, the sensible one: she knew that. So she suppressed the surge of loneliness. This was ridiculous. She *wasn't* lonely. She had a good life. Good friends, a job she enjoyed and two godchildren that were as close as she was going to get to children of her own. She had nothing to complain about.

As for that little flare of longing, she damped that down, too. Toby wasn't for her. He'd make the perfect dad: how could she ask him to give up the idea of ever having children? She didn't want to wreck his life, tie him down to someone who was going to end up hardly able to do a thing for herself. He deserved someone better and, as his best friend, she really ought to be helping him to find Miss Right, not selfishly holding onto him.

Without disturbing them, she walked quietly downstairs again. The minute Lydia and Paul were back from Canada, she'd do something about Toby. Find someone who could make him far happier than she could. Maybe fix him up with someone at one of the departmental Christmas parties. It was the time when people traditionally got together after all. And it would be her own very special present to Toby. She'd find him the love of his life.

# CHAPTER THREE

AFTER a week of looking after the children, Saskia was used to being in a family environment. She was beginning to enjoy it even. It was nice to come home from a late shift and not have to cook for herself or make do with a sandwich. Or to pick up Billy from nursery and be greeted with a big hug and hear all about his day on the way home. Or to see Toby walk in the door at the end of his shift, looking tired but giving her a genuine smile when she made him a coffee and sat down to eat with him.

She could almost—*almost*—see the point of getting married and sharing her life.

But one evening, when she was feeding Helena, the baby turned her face away and fussed.

'Everything OK?' Toby asked, clearly seeing the worry in her face.

'I'm not sure. She's not taken as much milk as she normally does.' Saskia frowned, and lightly pressed her fingers to the baby's forehead. 'I think she's getting a temperature.'

'There are lots of viruses about. It's that time of year,' Toby reminded her. All the same, he came over and checked Helena, too. 'You're right, her temperature's up. Do you know where Lyd keeps the infant paracetamol?'

'Second drawer down next to the kitchen sink. There's a child lock on the drawer, and the oral syringe is attached to the bottle with an elastic band.'

'Right.' He returned a few moments later with the oral syringe and a bottle of infant paracetamol. 'Rightio, little one. We'll get your temperature down.' Gently, he measured out a dose and squirted it into the baby's mouth.

31

'Give it a few minutes and you'll be feeling better,' he said softly.

Except the paracetamol didn't seem to work. When Saskia checked Helena's temperature again a little later, it was still up. She stripped the baby down to her vest and nappy and gently gave her a tepid sponge bath. The warm water would evaporate from her skin, whereas cold water would simply make her veins constrict and drive her temperature up even more. 'I think she'd better sleep in my room tonight,' Saskia said, 'so I can keep an eye on her.'

'You're planning to sit up with the baby all night and then do a full shift?' Toby asked, sounding shocked.

It was a lot to ask of someone who was completely fit, let alone someone who had a problem like Saskia's. She shrugged. 'It's a one-off. I'll cope.'

'Saskia, don't be daft. You don't have to take the whole burden. There are two of us. Let's take it in shifts to look after her.'

'And swap her from room to room all night? Hardly.'

'Let's share a room, then.'

She stared at him. 'What?'

'Come on. You slept on my bed often enough when we were students.'

'Crashed out after an all-night study session.'

'I'm perfectly capable of sharing your bed without having sex with you,' he said quietly.

Saskia glowered at him. What was he saying—that she wasn't capable of sleeping in the same bed as a man without demanding sex? Or that she wasn't able to make him want her, because he found her unattractive? Either way, it wasn't very pleasant, and she felt colour scorch into her cheeks. 'Well, thanks a bunch, Tobe.' Sarcasm dripped from every word. 'How to make your friends feel *really* good about themselves.'

'What have I said?' He raked a hand through his hair. 'I

wasn't getting at you. Just think about it logically. We're not students any more. We're both too old to stay up all night and then work all the next day.'

'Speak for yourself,' she said with a scowl. 'You're the one who's thirty-four.'

'And you're not that much younger,' he sniped back. 'We're professionals, so we're capable of looking after a sick baby between us without ripping each other's clothes off.'

'Mmm.' That sounded a bit better. Maybe that was what he'd meant in the first place and she'd just misinterpreted it. She'd already snapped at people today, angry and frustrated because her hands were stiff and achy and she couldn't do anything about it.

'So are we being sensible about this?'

'Yeah.' She sighed, knowing that she owed him an apology. Along with about half the hospital. 'Sorry.'

'Hey.' His fingers brushed her cheek, very quickly. 'It's OK. I know you're worried about our god-daughter.'

She blessed him silently for giving her such a great get-out. 'Yeah.'

And he was right about the bed. They'd shared a bed on countless occasions as students, when they'd fallen asleep over their books. After he'd qualified, he'd still let her study with him. Now she thought about it, she realised how tired he must have been—working long hours as a junior doctor and then studying with her. But he'd always made time for her.

Which was one of the reasons she loved him so much. He spent time with her. He was the first person in her life who had always, but always, had time for her.

And that was the real reason—the *selfish* reason—why she hadn't done anything about his love life. If she found him the woman of his dreams, he wouldn't want to spend time with *her* any more. Toby's wife certainly wouldn't want him spending time with his former best friend instead of with her.

What a bitch she was, putting her own needs before his. *You're going to have to give him up. For his sake*, she told herself.

Just…not until Lydia came back.

An hour or so later, Saskia settled the baby in bed between two pillows, took a quick shower, cleaned her teeth and was in her pyjamas by the time Toby walked in. Wearing only pyjama bottoms, she noticed. Since when had his shoulders been that broad and his chest so well defined? With just a light dusting of hair over his pecs, enough to be sexy but not enough to be offputting.

In fact, Toby Barker looked positively edible.

Quelling her panic, she tried to turn it into a joke. 'What's with the stripper act?'

He grinned. 'This is a lot more than I usually wear in bed, believe me.'

Toby slept *in the nude?* And he was telling *her* about it?

Then another thought hit her. Was he flirting with her?

No, of course not. Toby was like the big brother she'd never had. And she was like the kid sister he'd never had. Just the way it had always been between them. She pulled a face at him and climbed into bed.

He climbed in on the other side and checked Helena's temperature. 'I think it's coming down a bit.'

'Let's put her light show on, and see if she drops off.' Saskia switched on the little machine she'd brought in from Helena's room and turned off the bedside lamp. The light show played a soft lullaby and projected a series of pictures onto the ceiling. Various coloured stars were followed by a teddy bear in an aeroplane, then soft clouds which turned into the steam from a train driven by another teddy bear.

'This is great! I ought to get some of these for the littlies on my ward,' Toby said.

'I wouldn't mind one of these myself,' she admitted. 'More fun than a lava lamp.'

'It'd be good if you could get different pictures and different tunes—all you'd have to do would be to slot a different card in. A Christmas one with Father Christmas in a train, and stars and Christmas trees and holly. Nice soft lullaby versions of "We Wish You a Merry Christmas" or something. It'd be more fun than the piped carols they'll insist on playing on our ward from the middle of next week,' Toby mused.

'You've missed your vocation. You could've been a toy designer,' Saskia teased.

'Secondary career.' He grinned. 'I'll definitely get my own kids one. Then, when they've grown out of it, they can pass it on to me.'

His kids. And she couldn't have children.

'Saskia?'

Uh-oh. He'd noticed she'd gone silent. 'What?'

'That wasn't a come-on.'

'I didn't think it was,' she said stiffly.

'Besides, you're losing your touch.'

'I beg your pardon?'

'You haven't dated anyone for two months.'

Two months. Since the day she had been diagnosed with rheumatoid arthritis and the bottom had fallen out of her world.

She made herself sound bored. 'That's because there's nobody worth dating at the hospital.'

'No?' There was something odd about his voice, but she didn't dare look at him. She didn't want him to be able to read her face, guess what she'd been hiding from him for the last two months. It'd come out in the end, she knew that—and he'd be hurt that she hadn't told him. But she didn't know where to start, and the longer she left it the more afraid she was.

'No,' she said firmly, and concentrated her attention on the light show.


Mmm. Warm and soft and comforting. This was *nice*. Saskia snuggled back against the body wrapped round hers.

And then her mind jackknifed awake.

A body, wrapped round hers? Where was Helena? Was the baby all right? She struggled against the enfolding arms, desperate to get up and check the baby.

'Go back to sleep,' a deep voice mumbled against her shoulder.

A voice she recognised. Toby's.

Then she remembered. They'd shared the care of Helena last night. Except she'd fallen asleep and he'd obviously been the one to stay awake and look after their god-daughter. Guilt flooded through her. 'Where's Helena?'

'Asleep in her Moses basket. I checked her in the night— she was cooler and she was more likely to overheat be-tween us, so I moved her.'

Short, to the point and exactly what she needed to know. Well, *nearly* what she needed to know. There was one question he hadn't answered. Why hadn't he gone back to his own bed?

And then she realised something else. His left hand was underneath her pyjama top, cupping her left breast. His thumb was resting against her nipple. Her *erect* nipple.

It sent her into a tailspin. This was her best friend. She'd never, but never, thought about having sex with him.

Well, OK, she'd thought about it. But she hadn't actually *done* it. Apart from one kiss at a Christmas party, and he hadn't even remembered it the next day. If he had…

There was no point in thinking that way. It hadn't happened. And she wasn't going to wreck their friendship after all these years over just a little sex.

A friendship that would be wrecked anyway when he found the woman of his dreams, a little voice said in her head. So why deny them both the pleasure?

Common sense fought a brief battle with the little voice. And lost. Particularly when she noticed that his thumb was moving. Very gently, very tentatively—but definitely moving. Teasing her.

'Toby?'

'Mmm?' His voice was still sleepy. Yet he'd sounded very clear a couple of minutes before when he'd spoken about the baby. So was he putting on the sleepy bit, or was it the result of years of practice as a hospital doctor of being on call—waking up, dealing with a patient and then snatching some sleep whenever and wherever he could?

'Are you asleep?' she asked.

'Yes.'

Actually, his mouth felt rather nice against her shoulder. Skin to skin. Just where the neck of her pyjama top had slipped in the night.

'Is Helena asleep?'

'Yes.'

Was that her imagination, or had he just nibbled her shoulder? Experimentally, she wriggled her bottom against him.

'Saskia?'

'Mmm-hmm?'

'Stop fidgeting.'

'You're fidgeting,' she pointed out. And wished she hadn't, when his thumb stopped moving.

Though his hand stayed exactly where it was. So did his mouth.

Her call, then. Keep things as they were between them—

the best of friends? Or make this their swansong before she gave everything up?

The tingling in her fingers decided her. The tiny little sign, together with the numbness, that had hacked the bottom out of her world. She was about to lose everything. So, what the hell? He clearly wanted this, too, or his body wouldn't be plastered against hers, would it? She wriggled again.

'Saskia. I'm only human.' His voice sounded thick, tortured. 'If you push me…'

So she pushed. Simply by twining her left hand in his and moving his thumb.


He was dreaming. Definitely dreaming. Saskia Hayward was in his arms, in his bed, and she was inciting him to make love to her.

Or maybe he'd died and gone to heaven.

Toby was past coherent thought. All he could do was touch. Feel. Slowly, he undid her pyjama top. Button by button. Lord, her skin was soft. He cupped one breast again, and a whoop of delight sang through his head. She was as aroused as he was, her breasts swollen and full.

He was almost afraid to look at her face—please, please, don't let her be doing this out of pity, he begged silently—but when he turned her to face him, her eyes were dark and her pupils were huge with desire. For him.

And no way could he resist the fullness of her lower lip. He bent his head and kissed her. Lightly, at first, but then her mouth opened under his. Just as it had that time beneath the mistletoe.

He could have spent a year just kissing Saskia, but his body was urging him to explore further, deeper. He felt like a kid who'd just been let loose in a sweetshop, and he was planning to take his fill. And more.

The way she smelt. So sweet. Like roses after summer

rain. He nuzzled her skin, inhaling her scent, loving the softness against his own skin. His mouth trailed down her neck, down to her collarbone. He dipped his tongue into the hollows, and he felt her body arch against him. So she liked that. Good. He did, too. Smiling, he traced a line between her breasts with the tip of his nose, and heard her murmur agreement.

This was without doubt the best dream he'd ever had. So real. Everything he'd always wanted: Saskia making love with him. Her hands in his hair, fisting there when he opened his mouth over her nipple and sucked.

She was so responsive. Pushing against him, demanding that she pay attention to her other breast. In a decent dream he'd have super-powers and would have been able to do everything he wanted at once. He'd be able to kiss her all over at the same time, a riot of taste and textures under his mouth.

Now she was lying beneath him, on her back. He needed to know what was going on in her head. Did she feel the same way, or was he deluding himself? Maybe it would be easier not to know. But in the end he opened his eyes and looked at her. She was smiling. Inviting. And in her eyes he could see passion. Need. Love. Everything he'd always wanted.

He kissed her again, murmured against her skin. 'Saskia. You're so beautiful.' The most beautiful woman in the world.

And, since this was a dream, he could tell her he loved—

No. This *wasn't* a dream. She was really there, in bed with him. Kissing him back, tilting her hips under his, her body inviting him to remove the rest of her pyjamas and sink into the ultimate closeness.

This was such a stupid idea. Once they had sex, it would be over between them. For good.

But he'd had thirteen years of waiting. He just couldn't

wait for her any more. He needed her. Right now. Slowly, he splayed one hand against her midriff. She shivered, so he let his fingers drift under the waistband of her pyjama bottoms. Peeled them off. Rocked back on his haunches and looked at her.

He sucked in a breath. She was beautiful. More beautiful than he'd dreamed even. And his hands were actually shaking as he stroked her inner thighs. He wanted to touch her, taste her. Lose himself inside her.

But he had to be sure. He wasn't going to force her into anything. 'Saskia. We can stop now, if you want to,' he told her softly.

'No, we damned well can't.' Her hands were shaking as she removed his pyjama bottoms, stroked his buttocks, and her voice was husky with need. 'Touch me, Toby. Love me.' She offered her mouth to him.

There was something in her expression he couldn't read—was she crying? Or was it just that she needed him as much as he needed her, felt that same desperate craving that only one special person could satisfy? He bent his head to kiss her mouth, then slowly moved downwards. He took his time, rubbing his face against the softness of her skin, flicking his tongue around her nipples until she gasped and plunged her fingers back into his hair, pulling him closer.

Closer. He slid one hand between her legs and cupped her. Oh, God, he'd wanted this for so long. The heat, the soft silkiness. All he had to do was move. Nudge his thigh between hers. Let those long, long legs wrap around his waist and pull them both into paradise.

'Oh, Saskia,' he breathed, slipping one finger inside her. She was warm and wet and so very ready for him.

'Yes. Yes, Toby, yes,' she moaned, arching up against him.

He'd just shifted between her thighs, ready to enter her, when he heard a loud bang.

Half a second later, he realised what the sound was. The bedroom door slamming against the wall. *Billy.* Instantly, Toby dragged the covers over himself and Saskia.

'Uncle Toby, is it time to get up?' Billy asked chirpily.

'Uh, nearly.' He could barely string the words together, shocked by how close they'd been to getting caught.

'What are you doing?' Billy asked.

Uh-oh. This was definitely a question he didn't want to answer. 'Tickling each other.' Please, please, let the little boy accept that. He definitely didn't want to do a birds-and-bees explanation. Not now. 'Can you be a really big boy and go and get dressed?'

'OK,' Billy agreed happily, and left the room.

Toby flopped back against his pillow and looked at Saskia. 'Um. So this is what it feels like to be a parent.'

'It probably—'

'Shh.' He put one finger over her lips. 'We'll discuss it later.' Unable to resist, he rubbed his thumb over her lower lip. His vision almost blurred with desire. Hell, so near and yet... 'Later,' he croaked. If he stayed next to her for one second longer, he'd forget where he was and continue exactly where they'd left off.

Sometimes life was a bitch.

And sometimes it promised to fulfil all his dreams. He'd waited so long. What difference would a few more hours make? He leaned over to kiss her lightly. 'Later,' he said softly, pulled his pyjama bottoms on again and went to check on what Billy was doing.

# CHAPTER FOUR

Two choices. Saskia had two choices. One: she could get up and pretend this had never happened. Two: she could stay exactly where she was and wait for Toby to come back. Finish what they'd started.

Whichever way she jumped, it was going to be a problem.

If she got up, checked how Helena was and was showered and dressed before Toby came back, she'd spend the whole day on a slow burn. Aroused. Wanting. Wanting Toby, to be exact. The way he'd touched her had felt so good, so right. One finger hadn't been enough. She needed to feel him inside her. Needed him to take her right to the edge.

But if she stayed put…what then? Billy had broken the spell. Toby was out of the room, had had time to think about what they'd been doing. Time to realise it was all a huge mistake, just a physical reaction to a member of the opposite sex being nearly naked, in close proximity, when he'd woken from a deep sleep. Hadn't he said last night that he could go to bed with her without having sex with her? Hell. She couldn't face rejection. Or, if he didn't reject her, maybe he'd expect their relationship to change after they'd made love, and she couldn't handle that right now.

With shocking clarity, she realised that it *would* be making love. Not just having sex. With Toby, deeper feelings would be involved. And then, when it all went wrong, the mess would be spectacular. Hell. She didn't want to lose her best friend.

Slow burn it would be, then. She swiftly got out of bed

and checked on the sleeping baby. Helena's breathing was regular and not too fast, and her temperature was normal again. Good. So it had just been a virus last night.

Saskia's own temperature felt very far from normal so she made her shower tepid. Turned the water to cold, even. But it couldn't quite take away the warmth of Toby's touch. The way his hands had felt on her breasts, the way his fingers had teased her nipples. The way his mouth had felt on her body.

'Stop it,' she told herself through clenched teeth. 'You're not going to complicate things with sex and mess up the best friendship you've ever had. Got it?'

When Toby returned to the bedroom and found Saskia halfway through getting dressed, his expression was un-readable. And Saskia didn't dare ask him what he was thinking. Right at that moment, she wasn't sure she could handle knowing. Deliberately not looking at him and fo-cusing instead on putting her clothes on, she said brightly, 'Helena's temperature is normal this morning.'

'Mmm-hmm.'

'I, um, wondered if one of us should, um, stay with her today. Just in case.'

'It's easier for me to get cover at short notice. I'll call in.'

'Thanks. I'll, um…' Hell. She was never hesitant. *Never.* But it was hard to talk sensibly when your brain felt as if it had been turned to mush and your mouth definitely wasn't working in synch with your thoughts.

How easy it would be to leap on him. Push him back to the bed. Strip off his pyjama bottoms and…

No. It wasn't fair to Toby. She couldn't use her best friend to satisfy an urge—even though he'd been the one who'd started it. The relationship would go wrong and she'd lose him. In a few months' time, she'd need all the friends she could get. When she had to leave the job that was her whole life and find something else to do.

Her mouth tightened. 'I'll get breakfast ready while you're in the shower. D'you want scrambled eggs or cereals?'

'I'm not hungry.'

Funny how his tone didn't match the words. Because Toby sounded hungry all right. Maybe not for food. But hungry. Wanting. Needing. Just the same way she felt.

She hardened her heart. It wasn't going to happen. And, yes, he might feel sore about it right now, but their godson had done them both a huge favour. Billy's untimely interruption had stopped them making the worst mistake of their lives. 'I might or might not see you downstairs, then.'

'Mmm.'

Which told her precisely nothing. Don't do this to us, Toby, she pleaded silently. Don't try to change things. It can't happen, for reasons even you don't know about yet. I'd tell you if I could. But I can't.

Silently, she finished dressing and left the room.

A few minutes ago, it had been like all his Christmases and birthdays and red-letter days all rolled into one. Saskia in his arms, naked and aroused. Her words echoed in his mind: *Touch me, Toby. Love me.*

Heaven help him, he did. Always had. But when he'd first met her, he'd known there was no way the sexiest girl in the entire faculty of medicine would ever consider going out with a shy, speccy nerd. His options had been friendship or nothing. He'd chosen friendship, hoping that one day she might look at him properly, see who he really was and feel the same way about him that he felt about her.

Just as she'd seemed to do this morning.

If Billy hadn't walked in at that precise moment…

Well, it could have been worse. Three seconds later,

Toby wouldn't have even heard the door bang open. He'd have been drowning in Saskia's honey-sweet depths, oblivious to everything except her and completely unable to stop.

But they'd been interrupted. For long enough to let Saskia think about it and change her mind. How the hell was he going to cope with being just her friend after this? How was he going to cope, living with her until Lydia came back? But he had to. No way could he let Lyd down and leave Saskia to cope with everything on her own.

'Looks like it's going to have to be business as usual,' he told the still-sleeping baby. 'Pretending I don't feel the way I do. Pretending I love her just as a friend, as a sister.' And all the time he'd ache with wanting her, needing her.

Toby didn't come downstairs for breakfast. Well, if he was going to sulk, *fine,* Saskia thought crossly. He'd just have to get over it. He wasn't the only one who was feeling frustrated, not by a long way. But she managed to chatter normally to Billy, drop him off at nursery and do her shift at the hospital without anyone asking her what was wrong. She also managed to sort out the ward's 'secret Santa' present exchange—where everyone who wanted to take part took someone's name out of an envelope and bought them a present, given anonymously on the shift before Christmas Eve and usually unwrapped on the ward.

But she still couldn't help thinking about what had happened that morning, and she was distracted enough to have a near-miss on the way home. Her emergency stop left her bumper mere millimetres from the car in front, earning her a rude gesture from the driver and a blast from his horn. Hell. She really had to concentrate on what she was doing, not think about Toby.

Or *was* it because of Toby? A nastier explanation suddenly occurred to her, Was lack of concentration a symptom of rheumatoid arthritis?

'Stop it. Don't be silly. It's your joints that are affected, not the synapses in your brain,' she told herself sharply. But the doubt was still there. The panic. Maybe she'd missed something in her research into the condition. Maybe. Maybe.

She was in a thoroughly bad mood by the time she parked her car outside the cottage, only for her temper to collapse again when she walked into the kitchen and smelt baking.

Baking? Since when did Toby make cakes? He was more likely to buy them from the patisserie at the end of his road.

'We made Christmas cookies, Aunty Saskia,' Billy told her shyly, and pointed out the plate of star-shaped biscuits covered in blobs of icing, silver balls and sprinkles. 'Me and Uncle Tobe. We're chefs.'

'They're lovely, darling,' she said, giving him a hug.

'And we made you a special cake. A nana cake.'

A cake, for her? She didn't think anyone had ever made her a cake. Maybe one of the nannies had. But certainly neither of her parents had. She blinked hard to dispel the threatening tears. She hadn't cried over her childhood for a long, long time, and she wasn't going to start again now.

'Want some?' Toby asked.

*Cake, or you?* She pushed the thought aside. 'Thanks,' she said, not meeting his eyes. 'I didn't know you could make cakes.'

'We were doing a scientific experiment,' he said. 'How was your day?'

'Average. How was yours?'

'Fun.' He grinned. 'I spent this morning playing with Helena while Billy was at nursery and realising how many nursery rhymes I'd forgotten, and this afternoon chucking flour all over the kitchen with Billy.'

She looked at him, this time about to smile at the picture he'd painted for her.

Then he delivered the killer blow. 'I think I could get used to being a house-husband.'

The smile died on her lips almost before it was born. House-husband. Well, he'd never be able to take that role with her. She couldn't have children. And it'd get to the point where she wouldn't be able to work, wouldn't be able to contribute to the household budget. She'd be completely dependent on him, so he wouldn't be able to give up work. 'Best find yourself a career-woman, then,' she said, hoping that it sounded light but knowing how bitter it felt.

The cake was delicious, but it nearly choked her—she had to force down every mouthful. 'I'll tell Mummy what a good chef you are,' she informed her godson. She glanced up at Toby. His face was unreadable again. She knew him better than she knew anyone else. He was the last person she wanted to become a remote stranger. How was she going to fix this mess?

Somehow they got through the evening. When Billy was in bed, and Helena was tucked up in her cot, Saskia made some coffee. 'Tobe. We need to talk,' she said, handing him a mug.

'Mmm-hmm.' His tone was guarded.

'This morning shouldn't have happened.' Why couldn't she look him in the eye? 'I think we're both embarrassed about it. We got a bit carried away, that's all. So let's pretend it didn't happen.'

'It didn't happen,' he said tonelessly.

He agreed with her, then? Good. She smiled in relief. 'I love you dearly, Tobe. You're my best friend. You're important to me and I don't want to complicate things. Let's just stay how we've always been.'

'Sure.'

She risked a peep at his face. Inscrutable. Was he relieved, disappointed, angry? She couldn't tell. Or maybe he felt the way she did: confused.

Whatever he thought about it—and that remained a complete mystery to her—life seemed to go back to normal again over the next few days. She didn't see Toby as much as usual at the hospital, but she reassured herself that it was because they'd changed their shifts to make sure the children were covered. He didn't spend much time with her once the children were in bed, but again she knew he was busy, writing a paper. He had to do the work some time. Didn't he?

A couple of days later, the emergency department paged Saskia. She rang them immediately. 'Saskia Hayward, Maternity Unit—you called me?'

'Dr Hayward, we've had an RTA in—pregnant driver, suspected placental abruption.'

Placental abruption was when the placenta separated from the wall of the womb. Blood accumulated between the placenta and the womb, forcing the placenta to tear away even more. In severe cases, the baby wouldn't get enough blood and oxygen and could die. For the baby to survive, at least half the placenta needed to stay in place.

'Patient history?'

'Thirty-two weeks gestation.' So, if she needed to do an emergency Caesarean section, the baby had a decent chance of survival. That was good. 'The mum's having contractions, says she feels sick and faint, and she's very thirsty. She's complaining of abdominal pain, and her abdomen's tense.'

Not so good: it sounded like a severe abruption.

'What have you done so far?'

'She's on oxygen, we've got an IV line in and we've checked the baby's heart rate. It's low.'

'OK. I'm on my way down. I need a portable ultrasound,

six units of blood cross-matched, and can you get her bloods checked and let me know the platelet count, please?'

'Will do.'

'Great. And can you bleep the anaesthetist, please, in case we have to go straight to Theatre?'

'That's my next call.'

'We'll need Paeds as well—I want Mr Barker, if he's available.' Things between them might be a little cooler than usual right now, but he was the best doctor for the job, the doctor she'd most want to work with in this situation. They'd always worked well together, been a real team. That wasn't going to change.

'Will do.'

In the emergency department, she introduced herself to Pippa Fletcher. 'What we think has happened is that when you had the accident and your tummy banged into the steering-wheel, it caused your placenta to tear away from the wall of your womb,' she explained. 'This means you're losing blood, which is what's making you feel sick and dizzy.'

'Is my baby going to be all right?' Pippa asked, her voice shaky.

'We'll do our best,' Saskia reassured her. 'We may have to give you a Caesarean section and deliver the baby.'

'But it's too soon!' Pippa shook her head. 'I'm not due till after Christmas! I can't have my baby now!'

'You're thirty-two weeks, so your baby's got a good chance. I'm just going to do an ultrasound scan to see what's happening. Then I'll have a better idea of what we can do to help you.'

She felt a twinge as she operated the scanner. No. Now was *not* the time for a flare-up. She might have to do surgery in a few minutes. She forced herself to ignore the ache and did the ultrasound. 'I'm sorry, Pippa. I can see a huge clot behind your placenta. We can't reattach your placenta or stop your condition getting any worse, so I need to deliver your baby now, by Caesarean.' The abruption was too big for Saskia to use tocolytic drugs to control the bleeding or give the baby steroids to mature its lungs.

'My husband…'

Saskia squeezed Pippa's hand. 'You'll need a general anaesthetic, so he wouldn't be allowed in Theatre anyway. But we'll make sure someone brings him up as soon as he arrives, so he can see the baby and you as soon as possible. I can't leave it, Pippa, because it carries too many risks for the baby—and for you. I don't want you to end up with something we call DIC, or disseminated intravascular coagulation, which interferes with your blood's ability to clot and means you may lose more blood. I might need to give you a transfusion after the birth, too.'

When Pippa had signed the consent form, one of the theatre nurses gave her a pre-med and then the anaesthetist set to work. Pippa was wheeled into Theatre, prepped and draped, and the second that Pippa's airway was secure Saskia knew she was going to have to work fast. The longer it took to deliver the baby, the more chance there was of complications developing.

She ignored the warning twinge in her hands. There wasn't time to find another surgeon. She had to do it now. Through sheer force of will she performed the operation, delivered the baby and handed the little girl over to Toby.

'How's the baby doing?' she called to him as she laboriously sewed her way through the layers of muscle and skin.

'Flat,' he said softly.

Saskia swore under her breath. OK, so her hands hurt, but she'd still worked at top speed. Surely they'd been in time? They must have been. Losing a baby at any time was hard, but losing a baby in the run-up to Christmas… No. It was unthinkable. Of course you'd feel the loss always, but every time you heard a Christmas carol or saw lights on the tree, or wrote Christmas cards, or wrapped presents, the pain would hit home even more.

She flexed her fingers, hoping the ache would go away. This was the longest part of the operation, closing up again. If she didn't do it right, there was a risk that the scar would rupture if Pippa fell pregnant again. She'd always been able to do this kind of thing in her sleep—why was it so hard now?

'Are you OK, Saskia?' the anaesthetist asked.

'Sure, Ricky,' she lied. Hell. Now it was obvious to her colleagues that she had a problem. If she wasn't careful, people were going to start awkward questions. She just had to hang on until Jim came back. Only a few more days. She could do it. 'Just…you know. I hate severe abruptions.'

'She's doing fine—no sign of DIC or a PPH,' Ricky said reassuringly. PPH was a post-partum haemorrhage, where a mother suffered heavy blood loss after birth.

'Good.' Saskia gritted her teeth and kept working. This wasn't going to be a total disaster. They might not have been able to save the baby, but at least they'd save the mum.

And then she heard the sound she hadn't realised she'd been hoping for. A cry.

'Baby's back,' Toby called. 'Needs to go to Special Care—blood pressure's low. Keep your fingers crossed.'

'We will. Well done,' Saskia said feelingly.

'Hey.' He came over to her. 'You OK?'

No, I hurt like hell and I need a cuddle. But if she told him that, he'd want an explanation. She wasn't ready to give one just yet. 'I hate abruptions,' she muttered.

He put his arm round her shoulder and squeezed. 'We got a result. Don't be so grumpy, woman.'

Yeah. If you keep touching me like that, Saskia thought, my concentration's going to be shot to hell. How come a friendly hug, the kind of touch she'd always welcomed from Toby, could turn her knees to soup? At the same time, she wanted to cry. It was what she'd wanted most, a cuddle. And he'd done it without her even needing to ask him.

'Let us know how the baby gets on,' she said, hoping he'd take the hint and leave her to get on with her job.

'Yeah. Catch you later, Saskia.'

Teasing. Friendly. Just as it had always been.

But now it was different. She was so aware of him. Aware of every movement, every touch. Remembering the way he'd touched her in bed, his clever hands arousing her to the point where she'd been burning for him all day. This was playing with her head, and she didn't like it.

And her hands were really, really killing her.

How much longer could she carry on?

# CHAPTER FIVE

THE weekend was wet and miserable, which meant no chance of taking Billy and Helena for some fresh air in the park. The baby didn't seem to mind too much, but Billy was clearly missing his parents, getting decidedly grumpy and needed to let off steam.

'Leave it to Uncle Toby,' Toby said with a grin, and picked up the phone.

It was only when he pulled into the car park that Saskia realised where they were going. Ten-pin bowling. Toby must have booked them a lane. It was something she'd never particularly done as a student, and she couldn't remember Toby being a fan either. Still, it might keep Billy's mind off the fact that his parents were still so far away. Speaking to them every night wasn't the same as having them with him all the time, and Toby and Saskia were starting to run out of distractions.

Obviously Toby had done this recently, because he needed no help in setting up their lane—Saskia wouldn't have had a clue where to start. 'Billy, we've got something special to help you bowl the ball,' he said. 'And you're going to beat Aunty Saskia, OK? Now, watch me so you can see what I'm doing. I'm going to roll the ball along and knock over all those skittles.'

Toby, who never did sports, was a demon bowler? Since when? Saskia was prepared to tease him about it—until he got a strike with his first ball. Lucky break? Probably not, because he didn't look in the least bit surprised.

'Have you been practising this on the sly?' she asked suspiciously.

Toby grinned. 'Didn't I tell you I'm our ward champion?'

'No.' Though maybe he had and she hadn't been listening. Maybe that's where he'd learned to do it, on his ward's social nights out.

'Rightio, Billy.' Toby pressed a button and the bumper bars came up. 'This means you won't get your ball in the gutter,' he said. Then he set up a ramp, so all Billy had to do was push the ball down. It rolled very, very slowly, and knocked down eight pins. 'Look at that! What a champ.'

Billy giggled with delight. 'They fell down!' His second ball knocked down the remaining pins, and he did a little dance next to the ramp. 'Your turn, Aunty Saskia.'

Saskia's first ball went straight into the gutter. Her own fault, for choosing a ball that was too heavy, she thought. But a lighter one didn't help on her second try: again, it went straight into the gutter.

'Out for a duck on your first frame.' Toby winked at her as the duck waddled across the screen at the top of their lane. 'Never mind, Saskia.'

By halfway through the first game, Saskia knew it was too much for her. She'd only managed to knock down six pins in all the time she'd been playing. Her hands were starting to ache. She flexed her fingers surreptitiously, but it didn't make much difference. When she virtually dropped her next ball, she was sure everyone was staring at the idiot who'd made the loud clunk, and flushed deeply.

'Look, this is a boys' thing,' she said. 'I'll watch. And Helena's bound to wake up in a minute. I'll need to feed her.'

Toby's raised eyebrow said he didn't believe her.

She folded her arms. 'It's just not my sort of thing.' She could push herself through to the end, but she knew she'd suffer for it later. What was the point?

'Saskia, I'll put the bumper bars up on your turn so it's a bit more fun for you.'

She shook her head. 'I'm not a baby, so don't treat me like one. I'll just watch, OK?'

Toby frowned. This wasn't like Saskia. She'd been a bit strange with him ever since the morning they'd so nearly made love, but lately things had been getting back to near normal. She wasn't the over-competitive sort who couldn't stand losing—at work, she was known for being scrupulously fair and making sure the nurses and her juniors got full credit for their work, rather than trampling over everyone in her ambition to get to the top. So why was she so touchy about losing at ten-pin bowling? Or was it just that the bowling alley had got their decorations up, and that reminded her of how much she was dreading spending Christmas with her parents?

No, probably not that. Saskia usually worked on Christmas Day, making sure the staff on her ward who had kids could spend the day with them. Something was bothering her, he could tell, but what?

'How about I help you with your technique?' he offered. 'I'll guide your arm, if you like.' Though it would be sweet torture, having his arms round her and not being able to touch her in the way he really wanted to.

'Thanks, but I'd rather watch.'

Delivered in a tone so cold, so cutting… This definitely wasn't like her. His frown deepened. 'Are you all right?'

'Why wouldn't I be?'

She didn't snap either. Unless…? The penny dropped. PMT. Honestly. He was a doctor—not a specialist in women's health, admittedly, but his training had covered it—so he should have spotted the signs. After this, he decided, they'd get in supplies of chocolate. Lots of chocolate. Maybe that might help.

\* \* \*

Except it didn't. Even one of her favourite films, a bucket of popcorn and an enormous supply of chocolate didn't seem to shift her mood. The smile didn't reach her eyes, and she seemed to be preoccupied about something. Something she clearly wasn't going to share with him.

Even when the weather cleared up the next day, Saskia seemed distracted, and she didn't argue with him in the park when he offered to push Helena's pram. Maybe it was the family thing, he thought. Saskia wasn't used to it. Yes, she'd been the first to offer help—but, even though he knew she adored her godchildren, spending time with them was nothing like living with them full time. Saskia rarely saw her own family—she might speak to her parents every couple of months. Then there was her Aunt Connie, though Saskia had said little about her other than that Connie whinged a lot and drove everyone in the family demented. If you were used to living on your own, living as part of a family with young children could be a shock to the system.

Toby adored it. If anything, he thought, it was making him broody. He loved the idea of taking his kids to the park on a Sunday morning, pushing the baby's pram around the boating lake and chatting to his little boy about the radio-controlled boats. They'd maybe build a boat together, paint it bright colours and call it after the woman they both loved more than anyone else in the world. *Saskia.*

But he knew he was kidding himself. It was clear Saskia really didn't want her own children. Didn't want to be part of a family. So maybe he'd have to choose between them: having Saskia, or having the big family he'd set his hearton.

If only he could have both.

Appropriate rest and exercises should help to minimise symptoms. Yeah, right, Saskia thought bitterly as she sat in her office, glaring at her hands. When was she going to get 'appropriate rest'? She couldn't expect her colleagues to carry her at work, especially as they were already one short in the department while Jim was having his hernia operation. When she was supposed to be taking a break, she was busy helping put up the tinsel and the tree in the reception area—she always, but always, helped with the ward decorations, so no way could she have bowed out this year without people asking awkward questions that she didn't want to answer. And she couldn't rest at home until Lydia and Paul were back. No way was she going to let her best friends down.

The thought floated unbidden into her mind. *Tell Toby.*

She pushed the thought away. Of course she couldn't. He'd be over-protective and drive her bananas. Plus, she'd have to explain why she'd kept it from him for over two months. She didn't have a reasonable excuse either. Just that she was scared. How pathetic was that?

For the first time in her life, she was unable to make a decision. Held back by physical inability to do something. And she *hated* it.

'Dr Hayward?' Kerry, their new young midwife, knocked diffidently on her office door. 'I'm sorry to interrupt.'

Saskia forced a smile to her face. 'You're not interrupting anything, Kerry. That's what I'm here for. And call me Saskia—we're not formal here. We're all on the same team.'

'Saskia.' Kerry still looked nervous. 'I would've asked Georgina, but she's in with a difficult labour. It's just…my mum's labour isn't progressing the way it should. She's fully dilated but I think the baby might be stuck.'

'Shoulder dystocia?' Saskia asked. Shoulder dystocia, sometimes called impacted shoulders, was a condition where the baby's shoulders didn't rotate in the mum's pelvis the way they should, so the baby could get stuck after the head was delivered. Pulling on the baby's head or putting pressure on the top of the mum's uterus could make the baby end up with neurological problems or a fracture. 'What's the gestation?'

'Forty-one weeks and three days, we think.'

Prolonged pregnancy doubled the risk of shoulder dystocia. Saskia nodded. 'Is the mum diabetic?'

'No, but she weighs eighty-three kilos.'

When the mother weighed over eighty kilograms, it often meant the baby was larger and the pregnancy was likely to last for more than forty weeks. It also meant that the mum had a greater risk of being diabetic—and babies of diabetic mums tended to have larger shoulder-to-head and chest-to-head ratios, meaning difficult deliveries. Overall, the risk of shoulder dystocia increased eightfold. Saskia sighed inwardly. 'I'll come and take a look.'

'Thanks, Doct—Saskia,' Kerry corrected herself swiftly. 'It was going to be my first solo delivery.'

Saskia saw the disappointment on the young midwife's face. 'Hey. You're supposed to get a nice easy one for your first solo—shoulder dystocia's a tricky complication, so this doesn't count. Don't go thinking you're a failure, Kerry. You've done the exactly right thing, telling me instead of struggling on your own until you've put the mum or the baby at risk.' And shoulder dystocia carried a particularly nasty risk: the baby could die from lack of oxygen.

'Right.' Kerry's smile was clearly forced.

Kerry introduced Saskia to Jenny and her husband, David. A quick examination told Saskia that the baby was indeed stuck. 'OK, Jenny, you'll need a bit of help delivering your baby, because the baby's shoulders are stuck,' she said to the mum, who was lying on the bed. 'What we'll do is change your position to make your pelvis a bit wider, and we may need to give you an episiotomy.'

'I really don't want to be cut,' Jenny said.

'Trust me, you really don't want the alternative,' Saskia said. 'Your baby's big, and the last thing I want is for you to tear badly. I'll keep the cut as small as possible,' she added.

Jenny looked unconvinced. 'My sister had an episiotomy and she had to have her stitches redone twice.'

Saskia winced. 'Ouch. I'm not surprised the idea makes you nervous, then! Well, I promise that's not going to happen to you. None of my mums have ever needed to have their stitches redone—not even once.'

When Jenny still looked doubtful, Saskia added quietly, 'Jenny, your baby's stuck—and there's a risk the baby might die from asphyxiation if we don't deliver fast.'

Jenny sighed. 'I just want my baby out.'

'Then, please, let me work with you on this.'

'Do it, Jen. Don't risk the baby,' David said.

Jenny nodded. 'All right.'

'Thank you. I'm going to manoeuvre you a bit here—but until I'm ready, I don't want you to push *at all*, OK?' Saskia warned.

'So what do I do?' Jenny asked.

'Pant. Kerry's going to help you—keep talking to her about how you're feeling, and she'll know exactly what you need to do next. She's good, our Kerry.' Saskia smiled encouragement at both of them.

'What about me?' David asked.

'You're our support man. Your job's to keep Jenny talking to us and hold her hand,' Saskia told him with a grin.

She put Jenny into the lithotomy position, flexing Jenny's hips with her buttocks supported on a pillow over the edge of the bed, and bringing Jenny's thighs up to her abdomen before giving her an episiotomy.

'I need some suprapubic pressure, Kerry,' Saskia said. 'Firm, please.'

Kerry nodded, and followed Saskia's directions as Saskia tried to deliver the baby.

'OK, stop now,' Saskia said. A quick check showed her that the baby's anterior shoulder wasn't yet under the symphysis, where the pelvic outlet was widest. She rotated the baby's shoulder and tried again. Still no luck. Hell. That meant she needed to rotate the baby by a hundred and eighty degrees. Which meant she needed her hand in Jenny's sacral hollow. Which meant her arm was going to get squeezed by a contraction—and that might spark off a flare-up.

A glance at the foetal monitor made the decision for her. If she didn't deliver this baby pronto, they could lose it. She didn't have time to ask someone else for help—besides, she was supposed to be acting consultant. The senior doctor on the ward. And if she couldn't cope, it would make Jenny panic even more, the panic would transmit to the baby, and the last thing they needed now was for the baby to be in distress.

'What's happening?' David asked.

'I just need to move the baby round. Jenny, it's not going to hurt, but it won't be wonderfully comfortable either,' Saskia warned.

Grimly, she performed the manoeuvre. It hurt like hell. It isn't that comfortable for Jenny either, so stop moaning, she told herself sharply. But, oh, it hurt. And her hands just didn't seem to have the strength.

After what seemed like eternity, the baby slid out.

'You have a lovely big girl,' Saskia said, clamping the cord and then bringing the baby up onto Jenny's chest so she was skin to skin with her daughter. 'Well done.' She smiled at Kerry and David. 'Well done to you both, too. David, do you want to cut the cord?'

'If I can.'

'No problem. And, Kerry, will you take care of the last

stage?' Saskia knew that if the young midwife delivered the placenta on her own, she'd feel that she'd taken an active role in the birth.

Kerry nodded. 'Sure.'

David cut the cord, and as Kerry started to deliver the placenta, Saskia gently took the baby from Jenny. 'I'll just weigh this little one and clean her up a bit,' she said, smiling at Jenny. She ignored the tingling in her hand, but her smile faded as she weighed the baby. Shoulder dystocia and the resulting problems with delivery could cause an injury known as BPP, or brachial plexus paralysis—nerve damage that affected the arm. It was partly caused by the huge pressures between the baby's shoulder and the mother's pelvis, and partly by the traction on the head away from the shoulder. And the little girl's left arm wasn't moving as it should be, which meant she probably had some kind of BPP.

With luck, it would be temporary, and Saskia knew that the neurological examinations would be more reliable in a couple of days' time. Now wasn't the time to panic—though she needed to warn Jenny of the possibilities. Gently, she finished checking the baby over, then brought the little girl back to her mum.

'Jenny, you had a tough delivery. And sometimes, when a baby's shoulders have been stuck, there can be some damage to the baby's nerves.'

'Our baby's all right, though, isn't she?' David asked.

'I'm sure she'll be fine,' Saskia reassured them, 'but I did notice that her left arm wasn't responding the way it should. I think she may have something called a brachial plexus injury—that's on either side of your neck, between your neck and your shoulder.' She gently touched the areas affected on the baby. 'It doesn't hurt her, but it involves a group of nerves that runs from your spinal cord through your arm, down to your wrist and hand. In your baby's case, it's an upper brachial plexus injury, sometimes called Erb's palsy. It means the nerves aren't working as they should be and it's affected her biceps and deltoid muscle— they're the muscles at the top of her arm—so she's not moving her arm properly.'

'Is it permanent?' Jenny asked.

'It's too early to say,' Saskia said. 'It depends how badly the nerves were damaged—whether they're just bruised or if they're torn. We might see an improvement in a couple of days—in most cases, you'll see an improvement within a month. There's a lot we can do to help, such as physio-therapy and water therapy. If she's not a hundred per cent OK by the age of four months, we can repair the nerves surgically.'

'And then she'll be all right?' David asked.

'She'll have a much better range of movements,' Saskia explained. 'I really can't give you a proper prognosis right now, because she's so little. But I'll have a word with the paediatrician and we'll run a few tests. They won't hurt her. I'm just so sorry. About two per cent of babies born after shoulder dystocia have this problem—we don't know until they're born.'

'If I hadn't been so silly about the episiotomy,' Jenny began.

'No.' Saskia squeezed her hand. 'Don't blame yourself. It's something that happens sometimes. But we can do a lot to help her, so try not to worry.'

Though Saskia herself couldn't help worrying. Had it been *her* fault? Had she put too much traction on the baby's arm—had the pain in her hand and that stupid loss of strength dulled her ability to judge how hard to pull?

She hadn't had much choice. If she'd left the baby much longer, the little girl might have died. But if she hadn't been so stubborn about continuing to work when she really wasn't a hundred per cent fit…

She'd have to resign.

She'd do it as soon as Jim came back. And, in the meantime, she'd hand over any cases like this to her registrar. She wasn't going to out any more patients at risk.


'Right.' Toby removed the obstetrics journal from Saskia's fingers later that evening. 'Spit it out.'

Saskia should have known he'd notice that she wasn't reading it properly, merely flicking through and pretending to be working. Even so, she decided to play dumb. 'What are you talking about?'

'Something's upset you.'

'No.'

He lifted her legs, plonked himself on the sofa and let her legs fall back over his lap. 'You're talking to me, Saskia. *Magnus amicus.*'

Best friend. Yeah. The one person she could talk to about this—but the one person she couldn't open up to completely about it either. 'Just had a less than good day,' she hedged.

'Lose a baby?' he guessed.

'No.' She sighed. 'All right. Actually, I'll need your professional expertise in a couple of days. Erb's palsy.'

'Shoulder dystocia delivery?'

She nodded.

'And it sounds as if you're blaming yourself.' He started massaging her feet. 'Saskia, it's rare, but it happens. It's not your fault.'

'I probably used too much traction.'

'Not necessarily. The mum's contractions could have caused it. Are we talking C5 and C6?'

'Yeah. Only the top half of the arm was flail—there was definitely movement in the hands and wrists.'

'So, the chances are the baby's going to be fine. It's probably bruising rather than avulsion.'

And if it wasn't? Whatever Toby said, Saskia knew it was at least partly her fault.

'I'll come and do some neuro tests the day after tomorrow,' he promised.

'Thanks.'

People begged for one of Toby's massages. Whenever he offered them as part of the hospital fundraising promise auctions, there was always a string of bids. She should be counting her blessings and relaxing into the pleasure of the massage, but she couldn't. Even though Toby was very, very good at it.

Or maybe *because* he was so good at it. It reminded her of the morning they'd woken up together—the morning he'd touched her much, much more intimately—and that wasn't something she wanted to think about either.

Why couldn't life be less complicated?

'How was your day?' she asked, in an effort to take her mind off it.

'I had a little boy in with AIN.' AIN, or acute interstitial nephritis, was when the tiny tubes taking urine from the filtering units of the kidney became inflamed. 'I'm waiting on some blood tests and I'm hoping it's caused by post-strep infection.' If the inflammation was caused after the patient had had a bacterial infection, there was a very good chance of recovery. 'There was blood and protein in the urine and his face was swollen. They're keeping an eye on his fluid balance.'

Saskia frowned as she heard the catch in his voice. It wasn't like Toby to be so affected by his patients. He was an excellent doctor, caring and thoughtful, but he always managed to keep the necessary distance.

Then she remembered. AIN could also be caused by other diseases—including infective endocarditis. Toby had had an older brother who'd died at the age of six from infective endocarditis. He'd only ever mentioned it to her once, on the anniversary of his brother's death. Saskia couldn't quite remember when it was but, if it was around this time of year, it was hardly surprising the case had upset him.

'Hey. Sounds as if you need a hug.' She moved into a sitting position and put her arms round him, leaning her cheek against his chest. 'Memories can hurt, can't they?'

'Yeah.' Toby was stunned. She remembered? He'd told her one night when they'd been students, when they'd both been drinking far too much red wine and he'd been maudlin on the anniversary he kept to himself every year, and she'd got him to tell her what was wrong. The fact that he was an only child and shouldn't have been. His elder brother had died, and the shock had made his mother miscarry—the double loss had meant she hadn't been prepared to risk conceiving another child.

Saskia had hugged him, held him close. At the time he'd been a millimetre away from tears. Right now he wasn't that much further away. Saskia had had a bad day, had convinced herself that she'd let a patient down—but she'd still picked up on his feelings and put him first.

Ah, hell. If the other morning had gone the way it was supposed to have gone, he could have tipped her back onto the sofa and made love with her, until they both forgot where they were and what a rough day they'd had. Lost themselves in each other.

He closed his eyes and breathed in the scent of her hair. She was in his arms and she was holding him—he'd settle for what he had. He couldn't bear it if she pulled away right here, right now.

How easy it would be, Saskia thought, to let her hands slide under Toby's T-shirt. Stroke his flat stomach. Feel his body shudder in reaction to her touch. How easy it would be to let herself slide backwards onto the sofa, toppling him so that he landed over her. And then how easy it would be to kiss him. Nibble at his lower lip until he opened his mouth, let her deepen the kiss.

And how unfair it would be of her to do that, when she couldn't offer him everything he wanted. All she could give him was a short affair.

She had to get her hands off him, right now, or she'd leap on him. 'I can think of something to take our minds off it.'

'Mmm-hmm?'

His voice sounded very slightly slurred. As if he, too, was thinking about it. Sex. Skin to skin. Good old-fashioned loving.

'A game of chess.' Her voice sounded thick to her. What was that movie where Steve McQueen had played chess with Faye Dunaway, but everyone had known it had really been all about sex? Uhhh. How to be obvious, Saskia Hayward.

'Chess.' She could feel the rumble of his voice against her skin.

'Logic,' she pointed out. 'We have to concentrate on the game, so we stop thinking about today—and if we stop thinking, we stop hurting.' She would much, much rather stay in Toby's arms, but she didn't trust herself to resist temptation.

'And the winner gets…?'

She had a couple of suggestions, but no way was she going to make them. 'Loser does the washing-up for the rest of the week.'

'Deal.'

'I'll get the chess set.' She extracted herself from his arms with regret, and stood up.

'I'll get the wine.'

'Not for me, thanks.' She was aware of his speculative

look. 'Too tired. I'll fall asleep,' she lied. She didn't have to give up wine with her medication, but she was feeling rough anyway and she didn't want to risk making herself feel worse.

Chess really didn't take her mind off just how sexy Toby looked—his hair ever so slightly dishevelled, that tight black T-shirt outlining the definition of his muscles and just the hint of stubble on his jaw. And how blue his eyes were when he was concentrating. A deep slate blue. She could remember those eyes turning smoky with passion. Desire. That morning...

'What?'

His voice cut through her thoughts. 'Huh?'

'You just moaned.'

She could feel her cheeks sizzling. 'You imagined it.'

His eyes said otherwise. He held her gaze and said, 'Check.'

Hell, her concentration really was slipping if he was putting her in check this early in a game! They were normally so well matched that they couldn't guess the outcome of a game. Hastily, she moved a pawn to get herself out of trouble.

Had she *really* moaned?

A throaty, I-want-to-go-to-bed-with-you-right-now moan?

Her whole body tingled at the thought. Oh, hell. The quicker Lydia and Paul came back from Canada, the less chance there was that she'd do something stupid. Like climb into Toby's bed and finish what they'd started a few days ago.

'Check.'

Either he was on form tonight, or she was severely *off* form. And he'd notice it, too. Just as she was about to move one of her pieces, her fingers knotted up and she ended up knocking four pieces off the board.

'Sorry, sorry.' She winced. 'I guess I'm more tired than I thought.' Please, please, don't let Toby guess the real reason why she'd knocked the pieces over.

She couldn't tell from his face, which was carefully neutral when he said, 'Maybe we should forget the chess tonight. Why don't you go and have a long bath and an early night?'

'Maybe you're right. I will. I'll just clear this up first.'

'Don't worry about it. I'll do it.'

'Thanks, Tobe.' She leaned over to kiss him on the cheek. 'See you in the morning.'

'Sure. And, as you were losing, you get up for the rest of the week to make the coffee.'

'Deal.' She hurried from the room, and the second that she was out of his sight she flexed and clenched her hands, willing the ache to go away again.

Toby put the chess pieces back in place, then carried the table back to its usual place in the living room. He'd been so close to suggesting that he join her in the bath and early night. She'd probably guessed his thoughts, which was why she'd almost run from the room. The sooner Lydia and Paul were back, the better. Because he wasn't sure how much longer he could live with Saskia and not do something they'd both regret in the morning.

# CHAPTER SIX

TOBY finished examining the baby. 'It's good news,' he said. 'The tests I did show that the problem's very likely to have been caused by bruising during the delivery. She may need a bit of physiotherapy, but I think you'll notice a great improvement in her range of movement in the next few weeks. I'll get her booked in with the physio, who'll teach you how to encourage her movements, but you can basically stop worrying.'

Jenny started crying. Toby gently brought the baby over to her, and Saskia sat beside her on the bed, stroking her arm comfortingly.

'I'm sorry,' Jenny sniffed. 'It's just...'

'You were worried sick, and now you're so relieved, it's natural to cry. Plus, your hormones are swinging wildly right now—you normally get the baby blues on the third day after the birth, so you're feeling like every other mum on this ward does at this point,' Saskia said. 'There's nothing to apologise for. Thanks for sorting us out, Toby.'

'Any time.' He glanced at his watch. 'Actually, I've got to go, or I'll be late meeting Lyd and Paul at the airport.'

Saskia checked her own watch. 'Mmm, and I've got to pick the kids up. I put a chicken casserole and jacket potatoes in the oven on the automatic timer, so you can be up to half an hour late—anything more than that, ring me so I can turn the oven down, OK?'

'Will do.' He smiled at Jenny. 'If you have any questions, I'm sure Saskia can answer them—if not, she'll give me a call.'

'Thank you.' When he'd left, Jenny looked at Saskia.

'I'm sorry, you've got different surnames—I didn't realise you were married.'

'We're not.' Saskia shrugged. 'Toby's my best friend. We're looking after our friend's children while she's in Canada—her husband had an emergency operation, and they're flying home today. So I suppose we sound a bit domesticated, as if we're a couple. But we're just friends.' She was *sure* she hadn't had one of those moony looks on her face when Toby had been in the room. Or, if she had, she hoped he hadn't noticed. 'It's nothing, really.' She smiled. 'I really need to get going, but if you need any help, just ring your buzzer and one of the midwives will come. They'll bleep me if you need me.'

'Thank you.'

Saskia picked the children up from nursery. Toby rang her from the airport to say they were on their way. Saskia was playing a game with Billy while keeping one ear open for Toby's car, but Lydia was quicker. She must have sprinted from the car, because the front door burst open before Saskia even had time to get up. She swept Billy into her arms and whirled him round. 'Oh, *Billy!*' She kissed him and swung him round again. 'I'm never going to let you go again. Not for a second.' She shifted Billy's weight to one arm and scooped Helena from under her baby gym with the other. 'My precious girl. How I've missed you.' She rested her cheek against the baby's head, breathing in her scent.

Saskia turned away. Lydia was always demonstrative with her children, so this shouldn't have bothered her—but it did. Because it threw into sharp relief the fact that she couldn't ever remember her parents being like that for her. And that still hurt. Not as much as it used to—Saskia usually managed to mask it—but enough to make her uncomfortable.

Luckily nobody noticed because Billy was chattering a million to the dozen, clearly ecstatic to have his parents back again; Helena was cooing and gurgling; Paul, despite looking pale and tired, was swapping terrible jokes with his son; and the house was filled with noise and movement. Saskia slipped out to the kitchen to put the vegetables on, and busied herself making a meal.

A happy, noisy family home. Just what he'd always wanted, Toby thought. The way Billy was chattering to his mum and dad and asking them all kinds of questions about Vancouver and what an appendix looked like and how fast the plane went; the way Paul cuddled his baby daughter, with a pile of cushions on his lap to take most of her weight so he didn't damage his stitches; the sheer love that you could actually *see* flowing between the four of them.

This was what he wanted. With Saskia. Chatter and shrieks of laughter from their children, and shared glances with his wife over their heads, promising that later they'd have time to concentrate on each other.

Though he noticed that she'd absented herself again. He knew where she'd be: in the kitchen, claiming that she needed to get the food organised. Every time he thought she was starting to come round to his way of thinking, she ran scared again. Somehow he'd find a way of showing her that there was nothing to be scared of. Somehow.

Toby and Saskia stayed for long enough to have a meal with Lydia and Paul and do the washing-up, then left them all to catch up on their sleep. 'We'll see you tomorrow night for swimming, Billy,' Saskia promised from the doorway. 'Yell if you need us, Lyd.'

Lydia grinned. 'I'm shattered—but I'm *so* glad to be home. Thanks for everything you've done, you two.'

'No problem,' Toby said, speaking for both of them. 'You'd have done the same for us.'

As if they were a couple, too, Saskia thought.

Except they weren't.

They didn't even drive home together. Separate cars to separate homes.

And it felt very weird that night, being back in her flat. Home. It was a lot smaller than Lydia and Paul's place, but it felt almost too big, she thought as she wandered round it. Echoey. As if something was missing.

*Toby.*

No. She didn't have the right to think that way. It wasn't fair to him. If she were any sort of friend, she'd find him the perfect woman and quietly slide out of his life, instead of being selfish and clinging to him.

Tomorrow. She would start tomorrow.


The following afternoon, after their shifts, Toby and Saskia picked Billy up and headed for the local swimming pool.

'All right, Billy—you're the shark and I'm the fish,' Saskia said, making a fish shape with her hands. 'Come and get me!'

Billy, supported by his armbands, launched himself at Saskia.

'Good boy, that's it—kick, kick, kick and stretch your arms out,' Saskia directed. As she spoke, she took tiny steps backwards so that Billy was still swimming towards her but she was still near enough to step forward and grab him if he got into difficulties. 'That's brilliant. Keep going, Mr Shark... Ooh, you caught me!'

Billy chuckled happily and wound his arms around her neck. 'Yum, yum!'

'That means it's my turn to be the shark and yours to be the fish,' Saskia informed him. 'So, unless you reach that number one on the side of the pool before I do, I'm going to eat you all up, little fishy!'

Toby stood watching them, amused and wistful at the same time. This was a side of Saskia he'd never seen. She'd make the perfect mother, playing with her son and stretching him just that tiny little bit extra without him realising what she was doing. Just as she'd done with Billy, getting him to swim an extra stroke or two each time they played the shark and fish game, giving him more and more confidence in the water.

'Uncle Toby, will you help me?' Billy called. 'We have to catch Aunty Saskia. You're a shark, too!'

Knowing that he really shouldn't be doing it, but unable to resist, Toby gave the little boy a wink, swam underwater and deliberately headed for the surface just underneath Saskia. She shrieked as he tipped her off balance and caught her in his arms.

'That's cheating!'

'No. It's teamwork,' he corrected with a grin.

One tiny, skimpy black swimsuit. That was all there was between his flesh and hers. Had they not been in a public place, he would have been very tempted to peel it off. To kiss every millimetre of skin he uncovered. And to make Saskia shriek again—this time in passion as his body drove into hers under the water.

Hell. He definitely shouldn't be thinking like this. He tilted his lower body away from hers, hoping she hadn't noticed his immediate physical reaction to her. If she had, he'd just claim it was a guy thing. Which was true enough—wouldn't any man be aroused, with Saskia in his arms?

He let her go again. 'Your turn to chase Billy,' he said. He took a back seat for the rest of the swimming session—until they were back by the lockers and Saskia fumbled her bags as she pulled them out. They hit the floor with a crash.

Toby rescued them, but a small brown container fell out of her handbag as he handed the bags back to her.

A bottle of pills. Prescription medication. As far as he knew, Saskia was disgustingly healthy. What was she doing with a bottle of pills in her bag? He picked them up and glanced at the label—and then his heart stopped.

Methotrexate.

He knew what that could mean. In itself, it was bad enough that Saskia was suffering from a condition that inflamed the layers of tissues that lined her joints, causing her pain and stiffness. But she hadn't told him about it, hadn't told him she was ill—and that *really* hurt. She'd cut him out.

Silently, he handed the bottle back to her.

'Thank you.'

At least she had the grace to look embarrassed, he thought, noticing that her cheeks were flushed and she couldn't meet his eyes. 'How long have you known you had rheumatoid arthritis?' he asked, trying to keep his voice as cool and neutral as possible, even though he wanted to shout and throw things and make an enormous fuss.

'About two and a half months.'

A lot of things suddenly became clear. Such as why she'd stopped dating. But there was one question he couldn't get his head round. The thorn that kept driving deeper and deeper into his flesh. 'Why didn't you tell me?'

'I...' She took a shuddering breath. 'Look, Billy's here. Let's have this conversation later.'

She had a point. It wasn't fair to make the little boy overhear all this. But they'd talk all right, Toby thought grimly. The minute they were on their own.

Toby managed to chatter to the little boy in the car on the way back from the swimming pool, but when they reached the cottage he refused Lydia's offer of coffee.

Which meant Saskia had to refuse, too, because he was driving her home.

He drove away from the village, then parked in a lay-by and switched off the car's engine.

'Why have you stopped?' she asked.

'So we can talk. Without interruptions.' Deliberately, he turned his pager off. 'You, too,' he demanded. 'I don't want a bleep interrupting us in the middle of this. It's too important.'

'But I'm on c—'

'I don't care if you're on call. Someone else can cover you for ten minutes if need be,' Toby interrupted. No way was she going to let her job get her out of this. He needed an explanation, and he needed it now.

She sighed, grabbed her pager from her handbag and followed his lead.

'So.' He folded his arms. 'Why didn't you tell me?'

'I…I didn't know how.'

He frowned. 'You don't usually have a problem talking to me.'

'This is different.' Saskia unclipped her seat belt, kicked off her shoes and drew her knees up to her chin, wrapping her hands around her ankles. The foetal position, Toby realised, but he didn't feel guilty. He just felt angry and hurt that she'd shut him out. Something so important, so life-changing, had happened to her—and she hadn't told him. Hadn't trusted him. Did he really mean so little to her?

'So what happened?' he asked.

She shrugged. 'My hands were a bit stiff and achy in the mornings. Sometimes they were numb. It had been going on for a while, and it was getting on my nerves. So I saw my GP about it, had a blood test and got the results I'd half expected.'

'Your blood showed traces of rheumatoid factor?' Toby guessed.

'Yup. So I'm on methotrexate and painkillers. Apparently, it takes anything from two to six months for the drugs to start working properly. So I should be back to normal some time soon. Don't worry, I won't weasel out of cooking a turkey for you and Lyd and Paul at Christmas.'

Something in the tone of her voice didn't quite ring true. Saskia clearly didn't think she was going to get back to normal. And it frightened her. He knew he should be gentle with her, but he was furious. Absolutely furious that she'd kept the burden to herself for so long when he could have helped her. *And* she'd put Billy and Helena at risk. Supposing she'd had a flare-up when she'd been looking after them on her own? Supposing she'd dropped the baby down the stairs, or had let something scald Billy?

'For the last two weeks, we've been sharing the care of Lyd's children.' He only just managed to keep his voice cool and calm. What he really wanted to do was grab Saskia's shoulders and shake her. Hard. 'Didn't you think it would have been courteous to let me know you might have a few problems?'

'I didn't have any problems.'

'No? What about the nights when you asked me to do the kids' baths?'

'I thought you'd enjoy bathing your godchildren.'

'More like your hands were hurting and you were scared you'd drop them,' Toby corrected her implacably.

'All right, all right. I was in the wrong. You know the truth now.' She turned her head away. 'There's nothing else to be said.'

'Isn't there?'

'What do you want me to say, Toby?'

*I love you* would do for starters. 'You shut me out,' he said quietly. 'Something as big as this…and you didn't tell me.'

'I'm sorry.' She raked one hand through her hair and faced him again. 'Hell. Tobe, I didn't tell you because I didn't want it to be true. If I talked about it, admitted it, then I'd have to face up to it. And I...' Her voice cracked. 'For the first time in my life, I don't know what I'm going to do. I caused Jenny's baby to have Erb's palsy.'

'No, you didn't. It's a well-known problem after shoulder dystocia. You *know* the stats—you're an obstetrician.'

'For now,' she said grimly. 'But how do I know I didn't get the traction wrong in the first place? I can't feel things properly, Toby. My hands don't work as they should do. Sometimes they're weak, sometimes they knot up. And I'm scared, I'm so scared that I'm not going to be able to do my job any more. How can I perform surgery or supervise a junior surgeon when I can't even hold a bloody scalpel? I'm going to be a liability to the department. If there's an emergency section, I might not be able to do it. And a baby could die because of me. A mum could die because of me.'

'It won't come to that.'

Her face was white, and her voice was shivery with panic. 'I don't know what I'm going to do without medicine. It's...it's all I ever wanted to do, be a doctor. Ever since I was a little girl I wanted to be a doctor, make people better. And now I can't. Not any more. I don't know what I'm going to do, Toby. That's why I didn't tell you. Because I'm so bloody scared, and I've never, ever been in a situation where I don't know what to do. I...'

She broke off, her body racked with shudders, and Toby could see that she was fighting back tears. He pushed both their seats back and dragged her onto his lap, holding her close and stroking her hair. 'It's OK. Everything's going to be all right.'

She shook her head, clearly unable to speak, but she obviously wasn't going to let herself cry the pain away either.

'You don't have to give up medicine completely. Just change to a different specialty, one that doesn't involve surgery. OK, it means you'll have to do a bit of retraining, but you love learning new things so it won't be a problem for you. Maybe you could be a GP,' he suggested. 'Bottom line, you'll still be able to be a doctor, make people better. Maybe you could do the antenatal care for your practice, so you won't be giving up all your training.'

'I don't want to be a GP. I *like* working in a hospital.'

Compromise wasn't going to come easy to Saskia. He wasn't sure she actually knew the word, let alone what it meant. But if she let him help her, everything would be all right. He'd make it all OK for her. His arms tightened round her. 'We'll work something out. You need to talk to Jim when he gets back.'

'Supposing he says I should resign? If the positions were reversed and I were the consultant, I'd ask him to resign because he couldn't do his job. There just isn't room for dead weights—not on our ward. Or on any other.'

'You're not a dead weight.'

'I feel like one. It wasn't supposed to be like this, Tobe. I'm Super-Saskia—the doctor who can do anything.' She drew in a shuddering breath. 'Except I can't, any more. And I *hate* feeling so weak and feeble and useless.'

He could see it in her face. The anger, the resentment, the disbelief that this was happening to her—that finally there was something she couldn't control in her life. All overlaid with panic, because she didn't know how to handle it.

'You're the least weak, feeble and useless person I know,' Toby said. 'Stubborn, bloody annoying and head-strong, yes.'

'And I hurt you.' Her eyes were huge and still filled with tears as she looked at him. She lifted one hand to stroke his face. 'I never meant to hurt you, Toby. I just… I didn't want to admit it to anyone, not even myself.'

He could see that now. And his anger faded as quickly as it had blown up. Replaced by a deep longing. The way she was stroking his cheek… All he had to do was turn his face and press his mouth into her palm. Kiss her fears away. But that wasn't fair. She was too vulnerable right now. If he made love with her as a way of comforting them both, she'd resent him for it when she was back in control.

Gently, he removed her hand from his skin and kissed her forehead. 'Come on. I'll take you home. You need some sleep. Tomorrow we can talk about it.' When he'd done a bit of research, knew what the best- and worst-case scenarios were, and could come up with some sensible solutions.

'Thank you.' She wriggled off his lap and fastened her seat belt again. Toby dug around in his glove box for a Bach CD—the music, he thought, might help soothe her.

They drove back to her flat without speaking. On autopilot, Toby climbed out of the car and opened her door for her.

'My hero. The perfect gentleman.' There was a ghost of sadness in her smile.

And it was that sadness that wiped out his common sense. He wanted to make her smile properly again. 'There's one thing you could do,' he said as they reached her front door.

'What?'

'Marry me.'

Silence stretched between them, as sticky as tar.

'Marry you,' she whispered eventually.

Oh, God, oh, God, oh, God. Why had he said that? She'd bolt for cover…

Except she wasn't bolting.

She was staring at him.

'Marry you,' she said again.

He nodded. There was a lump in his throat that blocked any words.

'I can't. You want six kids—and I can't have any. Not if I'm taking methotrexate.'

She had a point. He wanted kids. Lots of them. The big family he'd never had when he'd been growing up. Methotrexate was a teratogenic drug—in other words, it caused defects in unborn babies. Defects in limbs or the face, hydrocephaly or 'water on the brain', and even anencephaly or absence of the brain or top of the skull were known problems caused by the drug. She'd have to stop taking the drug at least three months before they started trying to conceive, and without the drugs her condition would progress.

But if the choice was having kids or having Saskia... He knew what he wanted. What he wanted more than anything else in the world. 'Marriage with no kids, then.'

She frowned. 'But you want a family. What would you get out of marrying me?'

Did she really not know?

Though he couldn't find the right words to explain. All he could do was gently cup her face between his hands, tip her chin so her face tilted towards his, then bend down to touch his lips to hers.

A light, gentle kiss. The kiss of a friend.

Except it wasn't enough for him. He ran his tongue along her lower lip. When her mouth parted, he took more. And more. Her hands were around his neck, her fingers sliding into his hair and pulling him closer. His hands were cupping her buttocks, pulling her into him so she was left in no doubt about just how much he wanted her.

And then he broke the kiss.

'Just think about it,' he said softly, and walked away.

# CHAPTER SEVEN

SASKIA stumbled inside, feeling as if she were stuck inside one of those glass baubles that were on sale everywhere at the moment—the ones you shook so that glittery 'snow' fell everywhere around a reindeer or Santa or a Christmas tree. Her life had just been turned upside down and everything was swirling round her.

Had Toby really just asked her to marry him?

Had he meant it?

And that kiss…what the hell had *that* meant?

Toby Barker didn't kiss her like that. He gave her gentle pecks on the cheek and sometimes on the mouth—safe, undemanding tokens of affection. He didn't kiss her with barely restrained hunger. He didn't pull her body close to his so she could feel his erection pressing against her, proof of how much he wanted her. He didn't nibble her lower lip until she opened her mouth, or explore her mouth thoroughly with his tongue.

Ohhh.

Her knees buckled and she slid down the wall until she was sitting on the floor, her knees drawn up to her chin and her arms wrapped round her legs. The slow burn Toby had started back at Lydia's was smouldering again. Desire licked low in her belly, a burning need that only one person's touch could quench.

This was all wrong. She wasn't *supposed* to feel like this about Toby. He'd been her best friend for thirteen years. Toby was safe, permanent, an important part of her life. If she changed that now, if she made love with him… Well, it would be the end of their relationship. She knew that. And she didn't want to lose him.

All the same, she couldn't stop thinking about it. Just as he'd told her to do. *Think about it.* He'd suggested that she should marry him, and had then kissed her. Either she was going mad, or he meant it. And if he meant it... Hell, she couldn't even think straight. What was wrong with her? She always coped so well.

Right now, she was as helpless as a toddler.

'OK. Break it down.' She ticked the routine off on her fingers. 'Shower, get chlorine out of hair, go to bed.'

Bed.

Bad word to think about after that kiss. Bed and Toby. Bare skin against hers. His mouth. Those broad shoulders. That flat stomach. The dark hair arrowing down to...

Uh-h. Lust shimmered through her.

'*Sleep,*' she corrected herself.

That wasn't good either. It brought back images of that night. The night she'd slept in Toby's arms, woken to find his body wrapped round hers and his palm flat against her skin, and her first reaction had been to snuggle back into his arms.

She was confused enough. Why had Toby had to do this *now,* add the extra complication she couldn't deal with?

'Shower,' she said through gritted teeth. The hot water helped to ease her stiffness, so she was able to wash her hair, too. She wrapped her hair in a towel, tied the belt on her huge fluffy bath robe and headed to the kitchen to make herself some hot milk. It might help her sleep.

'Might' being the operative word. It didn't make her feel in the slightest bit sleepy. Eating half a tub of premium ice cream, straight from the carton, didn't help either. What she really wanted to do was pick up the phone, call Toby and ask him to come over. Hold her. Stay with her until she slept.

Ah, who was she trying to kid? She didn't want to sleep. She wanted Toby to comfort her with his body. Skin to skin, generating heat between them until she stopped thinking. Stopped feeing confused.

And how unfair was that?

'Saskia Hayward, you're definitely in line for the Bitch of the Year Award,' she informed herself tartly. 'You are not going to ruin your best friend's life. From tomorrow morning you're going to pull yourself together and work out what you're going to do about your job. Then you're going to do the right thing, tell Toby there's no way you can marry him, and find him someone who'll be good for him. Someone who can give him all his dreams.'

Toby's phone shrilled. Saskia? His heart leapt and he snatched up the phone. 'Paediatrics, Toby Barker speaking.'

And then he sagged in disappointment. Not Saskia. A secretary at the faculty of medicine at their local university, wanting to know if he'd be able to speak at a conference.

Any other day he'd have been delighted by the professional accolade. Today there was only one thing on his mind. One person, to be precise. He mouthed all the right words, asked for written confirmation and put the phone down again.

Had Saskia thought about what he'd said last night? Would she call him? Would she say yes?

He flicked into his email. Nothing from her. Hmm. She was on an early shift today, he knew. She usually met him for lunch when they were both on early shift. He was tempted to send her an email, suggesting lunch, but he held back. It was her move. If she wasn't ready to discuss things with him yet, there was no point in pushing her. Worse than no point—she might come back with an immediate refusal. And he wanted her to think about it, *really* think about it, before she gave him her answer.

That morning—the morning that still haunted his dreams—she'd wanted him. Last night, she'd kissed him back. It would be good between them, he knew. And he'd take care of her.

Or maybe that was the problem. Saskia had always been so independent. No doubt she was seeing herself as a burden, someone who'd drag him down instead of being his equal partner. Somehow he had to make her realise that it wasn't how he saw her. Never had, never would.

He'd spent a few hours last night researching her condition. Worst-case scenario, yes, of course there would be days when she needed help. Days when her body simply wouldn't do what her mind wanted it to do. Fine. He was prepared for that. He'd help her because they'd be a team, there for each other. Sometimes she'd be stronger than he was, sometimes he'd be stronger than she was. Ebb and flow. In balance, *together*.

How was he going to get that through to her?

No emails from Toby. Saskia leaned back in her chair. That was a relief. She couldn't deal with him right now. The first thing she needed to sort out was her job. Jim would be back in a couple of days. She could hold on until then— the disease wasn't progressing so quickly that she'd be risking her patients if she stayed on as acting consultant until their consultant was fit enough to come back to work. But the disease *would* progress. She didn't know how long it would take, but when Jim came back she'd have to explain the situation to him. Offer her resignation. Bottom line: she'd leave before she *did* start to put patients at risk.

And then she'd have to find herself another career.

How, when medicine had been her life? Ever since she'd been small, she'd been adamant that she wanted to be a doctor. She'd never wanted to be a ballerina or a princess or a fairy, or any of the other things little girls said they wanted to be. She'd always—*always*—wanted to be a doctor.

She'd lived her dream.

Now it was over. Time to wake up and face reality. She had to retrain. Do something else with her life. Something that wouldn't fulfil her, but something useful to fill the yawning gaps of time in her life. She'd thought about Toby's career advice and had come to the conclusion that she just couldn't face working in another area of medicine. It would be like a constant reminder that she was no longer working in the specialty she loved.

Maybe she should follow her parents' lead and go into law. Maybe one of them could pull some strings and persuade a tutor to let her join a law conversion course partway through the year, by guaranteeing that she would catch up everything she'd missed by sheer hard graft. She *could* do it. It would be hard, but she could do it if she put the hours in. A one-year conversion course for the common professional exam, followed by a one-year legal practice course and a two-year training contract. Four more years of study before she qualified as a very, very junior solicitor, but at least she'd still be able to work, keep her mind occupied. Even if her heart wasn't in the job.

*Marry me.*

Toby's alternative snaked into her mind again.

She rested her elbows on the edge of her desk and propped her chin on her interlinked fingers. She could marry him. Only that meant he'd have to give up all his dreams. The family he wanted, the possibility of being a house-husband. If she asked him, he'd claim he'd been joking. But she'd seen the look on his face when he'd said it. He adored children. He wanted children of his own. Lots of them.

The drugs she was taking would affect her growing baby, so she'd have to stop them weeks before she conceived. Without the drugs, her condition would deteriorate and she'd become a burden—to her husband *and* to her child. With the drugs, she couldn't give Toby the children he wanted. Without the drugs, she could have the children, but she'd be in no fit state to give her babies the care they needed. Holding them, feeding them, changing nappies—they'd be huge challenges, challenges she didn't think she'd be able to overcome.

There was no choice really. She cared too much about Toby to do that to him.

More than cared. She loved him.

And more than just the love of a friend, too, she realised with shocking certainty. She actually loved him. The whole big deal.

She wrapped her arms round herself. When had that happened? She couldn't point out one exact moment and say, 'Yes, that's when I fell in love with Toby.' It had just happened. The more she thought about it, the more it felt as if she'd always loved him. Which was crazy, because she hadn't even met him until she'd been in her late teens.

But she loved him.

And she loved him enough to let him go, let him find the happiness he deserved. Find that happiness with someone else.

If she stayed in Sheffield, letting him go wouldn't be an option. It would be torture, for both of them—their paths would cross and every time her heart would break a little more when she saw him with another woman. And break even more if she saw him trying to be brave and carry on alone, unwilling to spend his life with someone else if he couldn't have her.

So she'd have to move. Study elsewhere. London—no, somewhere less easy to reach from Sheffield. Aberdeen, perhaps. Maybe even further north. When she started her new career, she and Toby would be in different parts of the country. She wouldn't see him at work, and she'd be too busy studying and catching up to see him in the university holidays. And she'd keep herself too busy to think about him, miss him. Too busy to think about the huge chunk missing from her heart.

It was the sensible thing to do. She knew that. So she may as well start now. Grimly, she opened a new email message and typed a swift, businesslike request to her father.

'Sorry, Toby, Saskia's in Theatre,' Georgina said.

Toby suppressed a pang of disappointment. You couldn't schedule babies after all. Her job had to come first. 'Tell her to page me when she's free. I'll shout her a bagel for lunch. The canteen's doing their Christmas special from today—Brie, bacon and cranberry.'

'Some women have all the luck! I'm happy to be her stand-in, if you like,' Georgina teased.

'And I'll be your stand-in for Brad Pitt, right?'

Georgina laughed. 'Ah. You've got the wrong colour hair. Maybe not. I'll tell her as soon as she's out of Theatre.'

'Cheers.'

But clearly Saskia was working on a really complicated case, because she didn't ring him and Toby ended up having lunch on his own.

Maybe he'd gone too far, too fast, last night. Maybe he'd scared her off. But he hadn't been able to stop himself. The misery in her face, the despair in her eyes—he'd wanted to kiss her better. Maybe he should—

His bleep interrupted his musing. He checked the readout. Emergency department. With a sigh, he made his way to the nearest phone. 'Toby Barker. You paged me?'

'We've got a paediatric case—Kit, our SHO, thinks it might be DKA.'

DKA, or diabetic ketoacidosis, could happen as the result of untreated diabetes. In children, it usually happened before the child had been diagnosed or if the child hadn't been taking insulin properly. 'I'm on my way.'

He'd talk to Saskia later.

'This is Mrs Bennett, and her little girl, Tara,' the SHO said, then introduced Toby to Mrs Bennett. 'Tara's been losing weight recently, been off her food, and she's tired all the time.'

'How old is Tara?' Toby asked.

'Three.' Mrs Bennett sat next to her little girl's bed, holding her hand and stroking her hair. 'She said this morning she'd got a tummyache and a headache. I was going to take her to my GP, but then she started mumbling and I— Well, something just isn't right. I know you must think I'm making a fuss...'

In Toby's experience, a mother's intuition was important. Often he'd seen a child who hadn't seemed that ill at first glance, but the mother had insisted that something was wrong—and the examination had always proved the mother right.

'Not at all. I always listen to my mums,' he said. 'Has Tara had an accident at all recently? Fallen off her bike and hit her head perhaps?'

Mrs Bennett shook her head. 'Not as far as I know.'

'Anything else that's struck you as a bit unusual?'

'I thought she was going down with something, because she's always asking for a drink—I thought maybe she had a sore throat.'

Polydipsia—persistent, excessive thirst—was a symptom of diabetes. Most children who developed diabetes were over the age of five, but Toby had seen figures showing the rise in diabetes in the under-fives.

'May I examine her?' Toby asked.

'Yes, of course.'

'OK, Tara. I'm Dr Toby, and I'm just going to have a look at you and see if I can make you feel better,' he said gently. A quick assessment showed that her temperature was up, her breathing was deep and rapid and her heartbeat was faster than it should be. He could smell the characteristic pear-drop scent of ketones on her breath: Kit's diagnosis was spot on.

'Mrs Bennett, is there a history of diabetes in the family?' he asked.

Mrs Bennett shrugged helplessly. 'Tara's adopted, so we don't know. Do you think she's a diabetic?'

'It's very likely. Can you smell pear-drops on her breath?'

Mrs Bennett sniffed, and nodded. 'I haven't noticed it before.' She bit her lip. 'Oh, heavens. I should have—'

'You wouldn't pick it up until this stage,' Toby reassured her. 'How long has Tara been a bit under the weather?'

'Three weeks.'

'Most new diabetics have symptoms for nearly a month before diagnosis,' he said. 'So, if anything, you've caught her earlier.'

'And she'll be all right?'

'Once we've got her metabolism settled down again, she should be. What she has is what we call diabetic ketoacidosis, or DKA. Tara's body can't use glucose properly, so her body's used fats for energy instead—that released fatty acids into her blood, which have been converted into ketones. The ketones are what make her breath smell like pear-drops.' He decided not to tell Mrs Bennett that, if untreated, DKA led to confusion, unconsciousness and even death. There was no point in worrying her further, when Tara could be treated.

'So she's diabetic?'

'I'll run some tests, but I'm pretty sure that's the case,' Toby said. 'You'll need to be strict about her insulin regime. The good news is, we run a diabetic clinic for children here, and we can also put you in touch with some support groups.' He turned to the SHO. 'Well spotted, Kit. What tests have you run?'

'Just a urine test, so far—it was positive for ketones.'

'Right. I need some bloods done, please—I need to check Tara's potassium levels, as a priority.' If her potassium levels were too low, he'd need to replenish the potassium before giving her insulin, or she could end up with a heart problem. 'I'd like a full blood count, and check Us and Es, creatinine, sodium, magnesium, calcium and phosphate levels. And a screen for infection, just in case we've got a virus or bacterial problem lurking as well.' He smiled at Mrs Bennett. 'I'm not going to give her insulin until I've got the bloods back, but I'm going to put her on a saline drip, which will rehydrate her.' Slowly, to reduce the risk of cerebral oedema—swelling around the brain was a real worry where DKA was concerned, and if they corrected her blood-sugar levels and dehydration too quickly, free water could end up shifting into the brain.

He checked Tara's blood pressure. 'Her blood pressure's a bit low, so I'm also going to give her some plasma to help normalise it. When I get the blood results back, I'll be able to start giving her potassium and insulin. This time tomorrow, you'll see a completely different little girl.' He smiled at Mrs Bennett. 'I'm going to admit her to my ward, and we have facilities here if you want to stay with her tonight. There's also a parents' phone for incoming calls, so you won't have to worry about getting through to the ward.'

'She's going to be all right?' Mrs Bennett exhaled sharply. 'We couldn't have kids of our own. We waited for Tara for so long... I can't lose her now.'

Toby patted her shoulder. 'Definitely not on my ward. I'm going to ask Fran Smith, one of my senior paediatric nurses, to look after Tara. I'll be around for the rest of the afternoon, and if there's a problem someone can always bleep me. So, please, don't worry.'

'Thank you.' He could see tears glimmering in her eyes.

'If there's anyone you need to call, there's a pay-phone round the corner in ED Reception. Unfortunately, we can't let you use a mobile phone here because it might affect the equipment.'

She nodded. 'I really ought to phone my husband—I told him I was taking Tara to the doctor's this morning, and he'll be worried sick that he hasn't heard from me.'

'I'll sit with her while you call him, if you like,' Toby offered. 'Is that all right with you, Tara?'

The little girl opened her eyes and just looked lost. Toby stroked her cheek. 'Never mind, little one. We'll have you feeling better soon. Christmas Day, you'll be wide awake and bouncy at three in the morning and want to know if Santa's been! Kit, would you take Mrs Bennett to the phone?'

'Sure.'

By the time Mrs Bennett had come back to the cubicles from the phone, Toby had set up the drip, done the first set of observations and done an ECG to check Tara's heartbeat. To his relief, there seemed to be no abnormal rhythm of Tara's heart.

'We'll take her up to the paediatric ward now and do all the paperwork upstairs,' he said, and enlisted a porter to help take the little girl upstairs. He nodded to Fran when they got to the ward. 'Mrs Bennett, this is Fran Smith, sister on my ward. Fran, this is Tara. I'm admitting her with DKA, so I want hourly neuro obs and fifteen-minute glucose checks. I'm expecting bloods back from the lab any minute now—I'll come and sort out the potassium then.'

He smiled at Mrs Bennett. 'Fran will be able to answer any questions you might have, and I'm on the ward if either of you need me. Mrs Bennett, Tara won't be eating or drinking by herself for the next day or so, but the drip will do everything she needs. As soon as we've got rid of the ketones in her blood, she'll be able to drink normally again. Try not to worry too much. She's in good hands.'

The lab results were as he'd expected. He wrote up Tara's chart to add potassium, and asked Fran to add potassium levels to her list of checks. As soon as the potassium imbalance was restored, he'd be able to give Tara insulin, then work out the right insulin regime for her.

A couple of minor crises on the ward, plus checking on Tara, kept him busy until well after his shift should have ended. He didn't bother ringing through to the maternity unit, because the chances were that Saskia had already left. All the envelopes on his desk contained Christmas cards rather than a note from her, and she hadn't left him an email. When he left the hospital, he checked his mobile phone—no texts either.

Which meant she was avoiding him.

He couldn't leave it like this. That left him one option. Facing her.

And he wasn't going to do it unarmed.

# CHAPTER EIGHT

SASKIA ignored the shrill of the phone and let her answering-machine pick up the call. It was bound to be Toby, wanting to know why she'd been avoiding him all day. She really didn't feel up to that conversation.

But as soon as she heard the first word after the beep, she recognised the voice and picked up the phone. 'Hello, Father.'

'Oh, so you *are* there, Saskia.'

Typical. Her father always managed to make her feel as if she were four years old and in the wrong. 'Call-screening,' she said. 'I was working.' Marcus Hayward, QC, would approve of that, she knew. She was making the most productive use of her time.

He didn't need to know what she'd been working on.

Her resignation letter.

'I received your email,' Marcus said.

'Good. And?'

'What's all this about, Saskia? I've been talking to your mother about it, and she doesn't have any idea either.'

He'd talked to her mother? But her parents had led more or less separate lives for years. Ever since she'd been small. She couldn't remember them talking at mealtimes—they'd always been reading the newspapers or case notes. They'd always worked in the evenings, and work had spilled over into weekends, too. Her mother wasn't a barrister—she was a solicitor, working in commercial law—so as far as Saskia knew their paths barely crossed at work either. When had they had time to talk? 'I just need to retrain,' she said.

'Are you in trouble?'

Yes, but not the kind you mean, she thought. 'I just need a change.'

He tutted. 'Why couldn't you have thought about this a couple of months ago? The courses have already started for this year.'

'It's only the end of November. I'll have missed a few weeks, that's all.'

'A few weeks is a lot in a one-year course.'

Not if you were determined. 'Catching up won't be a problem.' She'd make sure she put the hours in.

'I suppose you're bright enough.'

So grudging. Saskia's jaw tightened. *Nothing I ever did made you proud of me*, she thought. *Nothing I achieved ever made you love me, not even graduating at the top of my year. Even now, when I'm asking you for help, you're nitpicking.* 'I thought you might be able to help me. Obviously not.' she said coolly. 'Forget I said anything.'

'Saskia—'

'I'm sure you're busy, Father,' she cut in. Just as he'd always been too busy to help her learn to ride her bike, or look at a drawing she'd brought home from nursery, or take her to the park and push her on the swings. It still surprised her that her parents had both found time to come to her graduation. Or maybe their secretaries had nagged them into it. The same secretaries who no doubt chose her birthday and Christmas cards and gifts. 'Goodnight.' *And happy Christmas—not.* She hung up.

It had been a stupid idea, asking her father for help. Marcus Hayward was a Crown Court judge. Of course he was going to ask questions, want to know the full details before he acted. And the second he learned about her rheumatoid arthritis, he'd tell her that law wasn't a suitable career either. He'd couch it in terms of concern for her, but she knew what he'd really be worrying about: that she'd make a mess of things, and people might associate her with him.

Her mother was cast in exactly the same mould. Ambitious, focused solely on her career. Her number-one priority was the legal system. Her marriage and her daughter came much lower down. Antonia may have discussed Saskia's request with her husband, but she'd left it to her husband to make the call.

What would it be like, Saskia wondered, to have a mother she could have phoned and talked to about her illness? A mother who would have read all the information, joined the help groups and come up with a dozen different things to make her life easier? A mother who might think of some way Saskia could keep doing the job she loved. Parents who allowed her the warmth of calling them Mum and Dad, rather than the stiff formality of Mother and Father.

Ah, but there was no point in brooding about it. It wouldn't change the bottom line. Her parents never had been the sort to fill Christmas stockings with silly, fun presents. Everything had been educational, practical or bought by their secretaries. Saskia was on her own, and she'd better get used to it.

The doorbell rang, and she frowned. She wasn't expecting anyone.

Toby? He had a key, so he wouldn't have needed to use the intercom to enter the complex, but he was also polite enough to ring her doorbell instead of walking straight in. Then again, she hadn't returned his call, so he'd probably guess she wanted to be on her own and respect her wishes.

There was a second ring, this time longer.

'All right, all right, I'm coming.' She opened the door without bothering to check through the spyhole Toby had insisted on fitting for her when she'd moved into the flat, and her frown deepened. There was nobody there. Then her gaze dropped downwards. There was a box of chocolates, set in front of the door. A *big* box. Her favourites—rich and dark, organic chocolate with seventy per cent cocoa solids.

She heard a whistle, and looked up. At the end of the corridor, she could see a white hanky waving.

It was enough to dispel her feeling-sorry-for-herself mood. She couldn't help laughing.

Toby emerged from his hiding place and stuffed the handkerchief back in the pocket of his suit jacket. 'Truce?' he asked.

'Yeah, truce.' She had her best friend back. Thank God. Everything was going to be all right now. 'Come in. Want a coffee?'

'Love one.' He shrugged off his jacket and hung it over the back of a dining chair.

'Good. You can make it. I have something more important to do.' She hugged the chocolates.

'You'll be sick if you eat them all in one go,' he informed her, clattering around in her kitchen as if it were his own. Well, he spent enough time at her place. He knew the layout of her flat as well as she did.

'Yes, Doctor.' She ate a chocolate and closed her eyes in bliss at the hit of pure cocoa. And then dark, dark truffle melting on her tongue. Oh, yes. Just what she needed. Toby Barker, you are *wonderful*, she said silently. 'So how was your day?' she called.

'Busy,' he called back. 'I had a three-year-old with DKA.'

'Three?' She frowned. 'That's a bit young, isn't it?'

'Yeah. The stats show they're getting younger every year. I'm going to ring the ward in a couple of hours, see how she's doing.'

Typical Toby. He had a soft spot for his smaller patients. Especially in cases like this. She'd often known him make a quick call in the interval at the theatre, or nip out during the trailers for a film, to check on a particular patient's welfare.

'How was yours?' he asked. 'I take it you were stuck in Theatre for most of the day.'

'Something like that,' she lied. Though she was pretty sure he'd guessed the truth already.

He came back into the living room and handed her a mug of coffee. 'All righty.' He sat next to her on the sofa. 'We need to talk.'

'I'm not really in a talking frame of mind.'

'Tough. I am.' His lips thinned for a moment. 'Saskia, I'm worried about you, whether you like it or not. I'm not fussing—I'm just concerned.'

'You don't need to be. I'm fine,' she muttered.

His response made her blink. She couldn't remember the last time she'd heard Toby swear.

'I read up about rheumatoid arthritis last night,' he informed her.

She wasn't surprised. It was the sort of thing he'd do. In some respects she'd half expected him to email her a link to a couple of journal articles. 'Oh.'

'How fast is it progressing?'

She shrugged. 'I don't know. It's early days.'

'So you might be panicking about nothing. You might only have it mildly. It might be years and years before you're too badly affected to work as a doctor. And there are new treatments being developed all the time—the nasal spray that's on trial right now, for starters.' He took her right hand and gently ran his thumb and forefinger over each finger in turn, checking her joints. 'Does it hurt much today?'

A bit, but she wasn't admitting to it. 'No.'

'Good.'

He stopped checking her hand, but he didn't let it go,

she noticed. Holding Toby's hand was…weird. Nice, but unsettling at the same time. Because it wasn't the way Toby used to hold her hand, in the way that a best friend would. This was…different.

Ever since that morning they'd woken up together, things had been different between them. That kiss last night had tipped the balance even further. And she really, really wasn't ready to fall. It made her want to run; she only just managed to stop herself wrenching her hand back and bolting into the safety of her kitchen. Mainly because she knew that, if she did, he'd follow her and extract an explanation.

'Have you told Lyd?'

She bit her lip. 'Not yet.'

'Why not?'

'She's got enough to worry about right now.'

'Saskia, you've known about the RA for two and a half months, suspected it for longer. Paul hadn't had appendicitis when you found out, had he?' He released her hand and folded his arms. 'So I'm not the only one you've shut out. You've done exactly the same to Lyd.'

She sighed. 'I'm just trying to get things straight in my own head first.'

'Does it occur to you that maybe it might help to talk over ideas with your friends—people who love you and want the best for you?'

'You're nagging,' she warned.

He shrugged. 'That's what you do when your best friend is being unutterably stupid, Saskia Hayward.'

She scowled at him. 'I thought we had a truce?'

'Yeah. And you think I'm having a go at you.' He raked his hand through his hair. 'It's not how I meant it to come out. Put it down to low blood sugar or something.'

'You haven't eaten?'

'Only a Brie, bacon and cranberry bagel for lunch.'

Guilt thudded through her. He'd left a message with

Georgina that he'd shout her a Christmas special bagel. Obviously he'd eaten alone. 'Sorry. I was in Theatre.'

He didn't say it, but she knew exactly what he was thinking. *You could have called me when you came out.*

She sighed. 'OK. *Mea culpa.* I was brooding and not good company, so I…' She shook her head in frustration. 'Oh, just have a bloody chocolate, will you?' She handed the box to him.

He raised an eyebrow. 'You've made a fair bit of headway with this lot.'

'Yeah.' Chocolate always made her feel better. Well, always *had.* It wasn't having much effect today—obviously the phenylethylamine hadn't kicked in yet. Phenylethylamine was a chemical found naturally in chocolate, which combined with dopamine in the brain to produce a mild antidepressant effect. She'd read the research papers to prove just how good chocolate was for you, and had been delighted to inform Toby that the chocolate she favoured—dark and very high in cocoa solids—was the perfect tonic.

He took a chocolate, ate it and pulled a face. 'Uh. I don't get dark chocolate, I really don't. Give me white chocolate any time.'

'White chocolate isn't actually chocolate, *per se.* It doesn't contain cocoa solids,' she pointed out, but she took pity on him. 'How about I fix us some pasta? I haven't eaten yet either. I bought some fresh ravioli yesterday, and I think I've got some ciabatta bread as well as pasta sauce in the freezer. It won't take long to heat up.'

Uh. Now she was babbling. Any second now, he'd pick up on it and arrow in on the reason: she was panicking because he took hold of her hand again.

'Want me to do it?' he asked.

Guessing that her hands hurt, obviously. 'No. You worked a longer shift than I did.' Besides, if she was busy in the kitchen, he wouldn't be able to nag her about the RA. Or discuss what he'd suggested the night before.

*Marry me.*

The sensible answer would be no. She knew that. So why couldn't she say it?

To her relief, he let her hand go, and she scuttled into the safety of her kitchen. She rummaged in the freezer and extracted the bread and the tub of home-made pasta sauce, then filled a pan with water ready to boil for the pasta. But maybe she'd taken hold of the handle in the wrong way, because suddenly her wrists hurt like hell and she dropped the pan in the sink with a clatter.

'Saskia?' Toby was by her side in what felt like half a second. 'Are you all right?'

'I just dropped the pan, that's all. Stop fussing.'

He must have seen her flex her hands, because he put his hands around her waist and physically moved her out of the way. 'That pan's heavy, even before you fill it with water.'

She *knew* that. She'd bought the wretched pan in the first place! Cast-iron French cookware that was a joy to work with. Though obviously now she'd have to replace it with something much lighter. Great. Yet another pleasure that RA had sucked out of her life.

'Go and sit down. I'll sort it.'

He was taking over, and she hated it. She hated being weak and unable to do even something as simple as cooking pasta. Before she knew it, she'd be like her Aunt Connie, reliant on a meal delivery service and whining to anyone who'd listen how bad the food tasted and how it wasn't like home cooking, but she just *couldn't manage* any more.

Heaven forbid.

'It's my kitchen,' she said through gritted teeth.

'Yes, and you're in pain. I'm not going to sit there and watch while you struggle.'

Her temper sizzled. 'I'm not struggling! It's *my* kitchen, *my* flat. I'll do it, OK?'

'And make your hands hurt even more? What's the point?'

'The point is, I hate being treated as if I'm some kind of useless invalid.' Like Connie, who moaned all the time that she couldn't manage this, couldn't manage that…and the more you did for Connie, the more she wanted you to do. Maybe this was how Connie had started, letting someone else manage for her instead of mastering the problem herself. A gentle start to a very, very slippery slope. And Saskia would rather jump off a cliff than turn into what Connie had become. A needy, clingy, desperate burden. Everyone in the family felt sorry for her but despised her at the same time and couldn't wait to get away from her.

*Never.* Saskia would never, ever let that happen to her.

'Just get out of my kitchen, Toby,' she demanded. 'Now.' She could manage. She *could.*

To her relief, Toby put the pan down. Good. So he wasn't going to fight her.

But then he did something she wasn't expecting.

He put one arm around her waist and yanked her to him, slid his other hand round the back of her neck and jammed his mouth over hers.

# CHAPTER NINE

TOBY knew he was in trouble. Deep trouble. Saskia was having a hissy fit—and he'd just silenced her in the worst possible way.

By kissing her.

She was going to kill him, the second he broke the kiss.

But he hadn't been able to help himself. She'd looked so vulnerable and hurt and angry—and he'd just wanted to kiss her better. Not that this counted as 'kissing better' exactly. How could it, when his tongue was stroking along her lower lip, enticing her to open her mouth? How could it, when his hand around her waist had slid lower, cupping her taut buttocks and moulding her body closer to his? This was pure desire. His self-control had been stretched that little bit too far, and this was the result.

Then he noticed that Saskia wasn't protesting. She'd let go of her anger and frustration—at least for the time being—and was responding to the demands of his mouth, his hands. She'd untucked his shirt and her palms were flat against his skin, easing over his muscles.

They both had way too many clothes on for what he had in mind.

He lifted his head. Was it his imagination, or had her mouth clung to his for a second longer? Was that regret he'd just seen in her eyes? He wasn't sure and, if it was regret, what was she regretting? Was she sorry that he'd kissed her—or sorry that he'd stopped?

'Saskia.' He brushed his mouth over hers again, unwilling and unable to relinquish all contact. 'I don't want to fight with you.'

'I'm not fighting with you.'

'Liar.' Again, he brushed her mouth over his. 'I don't want pasta either.'

'Then what do you want?' Her voice was husky, and it sent a thrill right through him. He'd actually cracked her legendary cool. Unless he was reading this very wrongly indeed, Saskia was as shocked as he was by the heat between them. And just as aroused. Her pupils were huge, her lower lip was full and reddened, and—his gaze travelled down her body—her nipples were pushing against her shirt.

'I want you,' he said simply. 'Just you.'

Now was her cue. She could tell him to get lost. He was even prepared for her to say it. And maybe the sensible thing right now *would* be for him to walk away until his equilibrium was restored.

But what she did was to tilt her head back and offer her mouth to him.

His head swam. How could he possibly walk away when she looked so gorgeous, so enticing? He bent his head and kissed her again. Revelled in the softness of her mouth, the sweetness of her taste. Saskia slid her fingers through his hair, and Toby lost it. Completely. He picked her up and carried her to her bed, still kissing her. Then he let her slide down his body, pressing her close so she could feel how hard he was, would know just how much he desired her.

She gasped, and he took advantage of her open mouth to kiss her. Hard. She was still wearing her work clothes, a white silk shirt and a black skirt. No doubt she'd hung the jacket up earlier. Saskia was prissy about her work clothes. Her lined wool skirt was going to crease to hell— but he'd let the dry cleaner deal with that tomorrow. Right now, he wanted Saskia naked. Naked and in his arms. He unzipped her skirt, eased it over her hips and let it slide to the floor.

Then he caught his breath as he realised that Saskia wasn't wearing tights. She was wearing stockings. The hold-up kind, with lace tops.

He glanced upwards. She was wearing white silk and lace French knickers, too. And he'd bet anything that her bra matched her knickers: Saskia always, but always, showed attention to detail.

With shaking hands, Toby slipped the first button of her shirt through the buttonhole. His fingers brushed against the swell of her breasts, and he shivered. He could still remember how she'd looked, how she'd felt, that morning when they'd woken up together, and it made his blood thrum through his veins.

He was sure she remembered it, too, because her hardened nipples pushed even more strongly against the silk of her shirt. How he wanted to touch her. Taste her. Send her crazy with the same desire he was feeling.

He undid another button, and another. Then he pushed the soft fabric off her shoulders and rested his face against the curve of her neck. She smelt like heaven. Vanilla and honey. Her skin was so soft against his face, warm and inviting. He traced a necklace of kisses round her throat.

'You look incredible.' Absolute temptation in silk and lace. Did she have any idea that she reduced him to a gibbering wreck? 'I want you so much,' he murmured thickly against her skin.

'Now. Please, now.' She was shaking, fumbling with his tie. He ripped it off, not caring that it was one of his favourites. Nothing mattered any more. Only Saskia.

She undid his shirt, then flattened her palms against his chest. 'Ah, Toby.'

He'd waited for this moment for years. He'd thought it was happening a few days ago. And now... Any second now, he'd wake up. Alone. Wanting her. Wishing things were different.

'Toby.' The tip of her tongue pressed against the pulse beating in his neck. He shuddered, trying hard to keep himself under control. If he wasn't dreaming, if he really was in paradise, then he wanted to make it good for her. Make it worth the wait.

What happened next was a blur—he wasn't sure which of them finished taking off his clothes—and it took him three attempts to unclasp her bra. But finally her breasts were spilling into his hands, a glorious weight. He dropped to his knees, took one nipple into his mouth, and sucked hard. Saskia thrust her fingers into his hair, urging him on. And then somehow she tumbled onto the bed. He splayed his hands either side of her to take his weight, and kissed his way down her body.

'So beautiful,' he whispered against her skin. 'Ah, Saskia, you're so very beautiful.' In black stockings and white silk French knickers, she was every man's wet dream.

And—for now, at least—she was all his.

Who said gluttony was a sin? He'd never, ever have enough of this woman. He nuzzled her midriff, traced a circle round her navel with his tongue, and she caught her breath.

He smiled. She was everything he'd always dreamed about. All the years of waiting didn't matter any more, all the wishing and hoping. He circled her navel with his tongue again, and he felt her arch back against the bed. *Yes.* She wanted him as much as he wanted her. And she was so responsive to his touch. It made him want to cry, cheer and pray, all at the same time.

*Hallelujah.*

He lifted her hips slightly so he could ease her French knickers down. Then he slowly peeled off each stocking in turn, stroking every millimetre of skin as he did so and revelling in the way her breathing quickened and she splayed her legs helplessly.

She had beautiful feet. Toenails painted bright jade—typical in-your-face Saskia—and a ring circling the second toe on her right foot. It always amused him when he gave her a foot massage to see that Saskia, the needle-sharp professional and organiser *par excellence,* wore such girly jewellery.

He stroked her insteps, worked his way up to the hollows of her ankles, slid his hands up her calves. He bent to kiss the backs of her knees, then let his mouth drift slowly up her thighs. She was quivering as she parted her legs for him, he noticed. Desire? Or was it fear that everything was going to change?

But everything had already changed, the morning they'd woken up together. It was too late now.

He kissed his way down her other thigh, hearing her whimper as he teased her.

'Toby. Please. Touch me,' she begged. 'I need to feel your hands on me. Your mouth.'

Her voice was so husky, he could barely make out the words. But he did what she asked and slid one finger along her warm, wet heat. Like silk in a rainstorm, he thought. He wanted her so badly. But he'd been waiting for a long, long time. He wasn't going to rush things now. He was going to savour every second, fill his senses with her and drive her to the same pitch of crazy desire that he felt right now. He brushed slowly against her, forwards and back again, forwards and back again.

Her hands fisted against the sheets, gripped the cotton. Her teeth were bared, and she was panting. Wanting him.

'Now,' he said softly, and pushed a single finger into her. Her muscles clenched sharply round him, and she groaned.

'Now. Oh, now, Toby, now.' She tilted her hips, clearly wanting more.

He bent his head, and she cried out as his tongue stroked

against her. 'Yes,' she hissed. And then she called his name, her voice shuddering—just as her body was shuddering under his ministrations.

When she'd stilled again, he shifted so he could lie next to her.

'Um. I...' Her voice slipped into a purr again, and he gave a mental punch in the air. He'd done the impossible: he'd got her incoherent and unable to speak.

And he wasn't finished yet.

Right now, he wanted nothing more than to sink into her warm, sweet depths.

*Condoms.* The thought was like a hard slap in his face. Oh, hell. Why hadn't he bought condoms? He needed to protect her. Especially now, when she was taking methotrexate. They really couldn't risk making a baby—a baby who'd be affected by Saskia's treatment.

His throat closed. If he didn't make love with her, slide into her body in the next two seconds, he would spontaneously combust. But he couldn't be selfish about it either.

Tortured if he did, tortured if he didn't. This really wasn't fair.

'Drawer,' she said, as if she'd read his mind and knew why he'd paused. 'Condoms. Drawer.'

He should have felt jealous—she kept a supply of condoms, which meant that she made love with other men. Or had done, in the past. But jealousy was buried way, way beneath the feelings of amusement—his touch had clearly affected her to the point where she couldn't string a sentence together—and utter relief. At long, long last, his dreams were going to come true. All the way.

It took him one second to open the drawer. Another to remove the condom and rip open the little foil packet. Just as he was about to sheathe himself in it, she sat up. 'No,' she said hoarsely.

She wanted to stop? *Now?*

And then he stopped thinking as she took the condom from his hands and rolled it over his erect penis. It was the first time she'd ever touched him so intimately, and it blew his mind.

He tumbled her back against the pillows, kissed her hard on the mouth, and pushed inside her.

She wrapped her legs around his waist, pulling him in deeper.

He wrenched his mouth from hers. 'You're incredible. The most beautiful woman in the world.' And I love you with all my soul, he added silently, knowing that she wasn't yet ready to hear him say it.

Toby. This was Toby, who'd driven her to the point of hyperventilating. Toby who'd touched her, coaxed flame from her veins and made her babble incoherently as she'd come against his mouth. Toby whose powerful body was thrusting into hers even now, taking her back to that glorious peak.

It wasn't real. Couldn't be. Toby was her best friend, not her lover.

But there wasn't anything remotely resembling friendship in his blue, blue eyes and, God, he was an amazing lover.

His gaze was so intense Saskia could hardly bear it, but she couldn't drag her own gaze away either. It was as if he'd hypnotised her. And there, in those blue depths, she saw passion. A deep, consuming passion.

He wasn't wearing his glasses, she realised absently. She couldn't remember him taking them off. Or had he switched to contact lenses? When? She'd never noticed.

There was a lot she hadn't noticed about Toby.

Like how broad his shoulders were. How strong he was. He'd actually *carried* her to her bedroom. Stripped her clothes off. Touched her and made her beg for more.

Caveman tactics.

That sat so much at odds with the thoughtful, caring man who'd been her best friend for so long. But it had sent a thrill right through her when he'd taken charge like that, swept her off her feet and hauled her in here.

And how sexy his mouth was. She'd always thought his smile sweet, shy—even a little vulnerable. Right now, his mouth was dangerous. The mouth of a predator.

Toby didn't date. Well, hardly ever. So how had he learned to be so damned good at this? she wondered. Then she stopped thinking again as his body drove powerfully into hers, pushed her nearer and nearer the edge. She closed her eyes, wanting to concentrate on the feelings flooding through her.

'No.'

'Uh.' Why had he stopped? It took her a moment to find the words she needed. She couldn't think straight. Could barely remember *how* to speak. All she could concentrate on was his body, joined to hers, and how good he made her feel.

Finally, she managed to unglue her thoughts. 'Don't stop,' she begged hoarsely.

'Open your eyes.' His voice was soft, but utterly compelling. Demanding complete obedience. 'I want to see you. I want to see you watching me. I want to see the moment you come—and know that I'm the one who took you over the edge.'

His words were enough to tip the balance. She sighed out his name, and then she was splintering, splintering. Watching him, seeing his eyes turn smoky as he, too, fell apart. And it was the sexiest thing she'd ever seen in her life. Quiet, gentle Toby in the grip of a fierce, all-consuming need. Toby at a most private moment—a moment caused entirely by her.

She must have lost a chunk of time because the next

thing she knew the duvet was tucked round her, her head was pillowed on Toby's chest and his arms were wrapped round her.

'Where...?' she began.

'Dealt with.'

Incredible. The man could actually read her mind. Then again, they'd known each other long enough. He knew she was a neat freak. But she couldn't even remember him leaving the bed to go to the bathroom and deal with the condom. All she'd been able to think about had been the incredible sensations still running through her body, tiny aftershocks of pleasure.

He'd made her come twice and turned her completely to mush.

She had to get her brain back into gear. Fast. 'Toby...'

'Shh.' He laid a finger across her lips. 'Later.'

She knew instinctively what he meant. They needed to talk, but the minute they started to discuss the issues they both knew they had to face, this feeling of peace, utter contentment would be splintered.

Right now, it felt good to be in his arms. Warm and safe. Comforted. She slid one arm across his waist, her fingers tracing lazy circles on his skin.

He kissed the top of her head. 'Careful. I seem to have mislaid my self-control. Carry on like that, and...' His voice faded into a husky growl.

She turned her head for a moment so she could kiss his chest. 'I do hope that was a promise.'

He went utterly still. 'You mean...?'

She couldn't help smiling. Did he really think she wouldn't want to repeat something that good? 'Yep.'

'Then I'm all yours.'

'What?' She stared at him, not understanding.

He lay back against the pillows and shrugged. 'Do what you want with me, Saskia.'

He was giving himself to her. Completely. He trusted her that much.

It was an offer she really ought to refuse. But how could she, when she could feel his heartbeat against her cheek? How could she, when his eyes were blurred with passion and his mouth was soft and warm and she knew how that mouth felt intimately against her skin?

'Anything I want?' she asked, just to make certain.

'Anything.'

She shifted so that she was straddling him. 'Have you been going to the gym?'

'No.'

'You don't get pecs like this by being a couch potato.'

He gave her a shy grin. 'Like them?'

She chuckled. 'You're fishing for compliments.'

'Uh-huh.'

And not ashamed of the fact either. The shyness had somehow melted into mischief, and she found it very, very appealing. 'Yes, I like them,' she admitted. 'A lot.' She liked this new side to him, too, a side she'd never even guessed at. 'You feel good, Toby.' She brushed her hands lightly over his skin and noted that he shivered. Good. He'd just blown her mind. She was going to do the same for him. And how she was going to enjoy that power.

She bent her head and kissed him, nibbling at his lower lip until he opened his mouth to let her explore him. Kissing Toby like this was something she could spend a lot of time doing, she thought. There was something about it that made her greedy for more.

She broke the kiss and shifted so she could kiss the column of his throat. She was tempted, so tempted, to use her teeth—mark him as hers—but she kept herself under control. Just.

His eyes were closed. Such long, long lashes, she thought as she leaned back and looked at him. He was beautiful.

Why had she never noticed just how beautiful he was? She nuzzled his chest, the dark hairs rough against her skin. Licked his flat button nipples, making him gasp.

She'd never really thought about doing anything kinky, but right now she would have given a lot to have a mirror handy. She wanted to see Toby's expression when he finally understood what she was going to do. But, more than that, she wanted to give him the same gift he'd given her. She wanted to make his world dissolve.

Slowly, she moved southwards, following the line of dark hair arrowing downwards. Toby suddenly went very, very still, as if he'd realised what she was going to do but didn't believe it was really going to happen.

Believe me, sweetheart, it is, she thought with a smile, then opened her mouth over him.

His sigh of pleasure sent a thrill through her. She concentrated on what she was doing, intent on sending Toby straight to nirvana. His hands tangled in her hair, and he murmured her name over and over again, his voice shaking and his body moving involuntary beneath her as he lost control.

Then she realised that he was saying something to her. Every word was an effort, and he was almost hyperventilating in between each word. 'Saskia, if you don't stop now…'

She was tempted to ignore him and carry on, but she didn't want to shock him. She wanted to delight him. So she stopped, shifted so that she was straddling him again.

His eyes were open again, and his pupils were so huge that his eyes looked almost black. Shock, desire and disbelief skittered over his face; she leaned down and kissed him. 'You started this,' she reminded him. 'You were the one with the caveman tactics.'

'Uh.' He was clearly having difficulty stringing words

together. Just like she'd had, earlier. And it thrilled her to think that her touch could do that to him.

'You win,' he breathed.

'No.' She reached over to the open drawer for another condom, and smiled. 'No. We both win.'

# CHAPTER TEN

TONIGHT was a night neither of them would ever forget, Saskia thought. And she couldn't ever remember anything being this good before.

Toby was an incredible lover. She still hadn't worked out how or where he'd become so skilled—she couldn't even remember the name of his last girlfriend or what she looked like, let alone when it had been. But Saskia realised that, for the first time in her life, she hadn't just had sex with a boyfriend.

She'd made love.

With Toby.

Which was why this was going to be so hard to stop. For the first time her mind and her heart had been involved, not just her body. In the past a brief fling had been enough to keep her satisfied for months. She'd dated a lot, admittedly, but very few of her men made it past a kiss. Even fewer made it to a second invitation to her bed.

Toby was different. They'd already made love twice, and no way was she letting him out of her bed before they'd made love at least once more. Even though the sensible part of her knew they should never have gone to bed together in the first place.

'You're brooding,' Toby said softly, stroking her hair.

'Am not,' she lied.

Then her stomach rumbled, and he chuckled. 'You need feeding. Problem is, I can't move.'

'Neither can I.' It wasn't strictly true. She could: she just didn't want to. Didn't want to move a single millimetre away from him. She had a feeling it was the same for him, too.

'We could be really decadent. We could order pizza and eat it in bed,' he suggested.

'Are you about to suggest something...piquant?' she teased.

'No. I'd need melted chocolate and strawberries for that,' he teased back.

Ohhh. The idea made her head spin. 'I have chocolate.' The words came out before she could stop them.

He laughed. 'Maybe another time.' Then his voice changed—became softer, huskier. 'Let me stay with you tonight, Saskia. I want to sleep with you in my arms.'

She really ought to refuse. She'd never let anyone stay the night, ever. Starting now wasn't an option. It would be just one night, and tomorrow everything would be different...and Toby would be even more hurt, because by letting him stay she was letting him hope that they had a future. She really didn't want to mess up his life.

She looked up at him, and her heart contracted. He looked so vulnerable. She was supposed to be saying no, but how could she trample over his feelings and hurt him now by refusing to let him stay with her? It would be like kicking a newborn puppy. She just couldn't do it.

So, tonight, they'd fall asleep in each other's arms. Besides, a corner of her mind whispered, she wanted one night to remember. One night of memories so hot that they'd keep her warm for the rest of her life. One night of happiness, before her life came crashing back to the black hole it was going to be for the rest of her days.

'Saskia?'

She nodded. 'OK. Stay with me tonight.'

He leaned over and kissed the tip of her nose. 'Thank you.'

She had to stop him saying it. Saying the words she

could see so clearly in his eyes. *I love you.* There was no future in it, and she couldn't say it back, so it wasn't fair to let him say the words.

There was only one way she could think of to stop him. She slid her arms around his neck and pulled his mouth down to hers.

This time their love-making was slow, tender. Toby was telling her with his body what she'd refused to let him tell her in words. Each kiss, each caress was a declaration of love. She matched him kiss for kiss, touch for touch. This time, when they climaxed, he pressed his cheek against hers. Cherishing her. And she wasn't sure if the dampness on his skin came from his eyes or her own.

Some time later, Toby nuzzled her cheek. 'What happened to the pizza, then, Dr Hayward?'

'You distracted me before I could order it.' She cuddled into him. 'Any preferences?'

'Apart from you, you mean?' He dropped a kiss on her hair. 'No. Anything.'

She reached out for the cordless phone on her bedside cabinet, pressed a button and waited for the number to ring.

'I don't believe you've got a pizza place on speed dial!' he teased. 'Dr ''I cook everything with my own fair hands and only buy certified organic food'' Hayward is a secret junk food addict, then?'

She pulled a face at him. 'Of course I'm not. These piz-zas are made by genuine Italians,' she informed him. 'So they're as good as home-made. Probably better.' She flapped her hand at him to tell him that her call had been answered and she didn't want him to interrupt her, then ordered a large *quattro formaggi* pizza. 'It'll be here in forty minutes,' she told him when she'd hung up.

'Forty minutes?' He looked shocked.

'Mmm. I told you, it's home-made. It'll be made from

scratch. So it's not like calling a fast-food joint or sticking a shop-bought pizza into the oven.'

'Forty minutes.' He gave her a very naughty grin. 'I can think of something I can do in forty minutes.'

'Oh, yes?' Lust shimmered through her. Again? *Oh, yes.*

He smiled. 'Can I use your phone, please?'

Oh. So he hadn't meant making love to her again. Either he'd been teasing her, or she'd misread him completely. She smothered the prickle of disappointment. 'Sure.' She handed the phone to him.

He lifted her slightly, shifted the pillows and plumped them so he could recline back on them, and pulled Saskia onto his lap. He held her close, cuddling her as he dialled a number he obviously knew by heart.

'Fran? Hi, it's Toby. I just thought I'd give you a quick ring about Tara. How's she doing?'

When Saskia realised who he was calling and why, she thought her heart was going to break. Toby cared enough about his tiny patients to check on their progress—even in the middle of an evening he knew meant everything to him. This warm, sensitive, wonderful man had offered himself to her. And she wanted him. She wanted him so badly.

But she couldn't have him. She couldn't drag him down into the abyss with her. Somehow, she was going to have to find the strength to let him go.

Somehow.

The alarm shrilled. Toby reached out to silence it, but his hand met nothing. The clock wasn't where it should have been. And, come to think of it, it didn't sound like his alarm.

When the alarm continued ringing, he suddenly snapped back to the present and realised where he was.

Saskia's bed.

Except Saskia wasn't where he'd expected her to be, curled asleep in his arms.

Uneasily, he opened his eyes, sat up, then reached across to turn off the alarm clock. Where was she? He distinctly remembered falling asleep with his arms wrapped around her and hers wrapped around him. There was a dent in the pillow that told him she'd spent the entire night next to him. But when he put out a hand to touch the pillow, it felt cold.

She'd clearly woken a long time before he had, had got up without waking him, and—hell, hell and treble hell—she'd had time to think.

Which was a problem. If she'd only follow her heart for once, instead of her head, everything would be OK. But, knowing Saskia, she'd decided that because she had rheumatoid arthritis and life might get tough in the future, Toby was better off without her. Once she'd got an idea in her head, it was near-impossible to get her to shift her viewpoint. She was the most stubborn woman he'd ever met.

But he wasn't giving up on her without a fight.

Last night, she'd dissolved in his arms. She'd refused to let him tell her he loved her, but she'd let him show her with his body. And she'd given just as much as she'd taken. Toby was pretty sure she felt exactly the same way he did.

It was just a question of getting her to admit it.

*Just.* Ha. Saskia was the queen of stubbornness.

He pulled his boxer shorts on and went in search of her. He found her in the kitchen, reading a medical journal and sipping coffee. In a perfectly neat kitchen—the pizza box from last night was gone and the pan of water she'd left in the sink had been washed up, dried and put away.

And her body was sending him definite 'keep off' signals.

'Morning,' he said.

She looked up and gave him a bright smile. A bright,

brittle smile that didn't reach her eyes, though only some-one who knew her as well as Toby would be able to tell that. 'Morning. Did you sleep well?'

Ah, so this was the plan. Bright, breezy hostess greets guest over breakfast and pretends last night didn't happen. OK. He'd play it her way—for now. 'Fine. Did you?'

'Fine.'

It begged the question: if she'd slept so well, why was she up so early?

'There's plenty of hot water. Help yourself to a shower. You know where the towels are.'

For a moment, Toby considered picking her up and drag-ging her into the shower with him. Peeling off that prissy business suit—a navy wool one this time—and making her cry out as she'd done last night. Making her eyes heavy and glazed with passion, instead of that bright, shiny, brittle look. Kissing her until her lipstick was gone and her mouth was reddened and swollen with passion.

But, if he did, he knew that the second their love-making was over she'd retreat back into her shell.

He switched tactics. 'Sure. Um, are you on an early to-day?'

'No.'

So why was she up and dressed at this time of the morn-ing? Why had she set her alarm? She didn't have to be at the hospital for hours yet.

'Are you?' she asked.

'No. A late.' Just as well. The clothes he'd worn last night must be extremely creased. No way could he walk onto the ward wearing them. Not without a lot of comment and a lot of speculation, which would make Saskia put yet another wall round her. At least being on a late meant he could go home and change.

'I'll give you ten minutes to shower and dress, then the ciabatta bread will be ready.'

The bread they hadn't got round to eating last night, because they'd been making love. But, to hear her speak, it was as if Toby had just stayed overnight because they'd been out somewhere and it had been late by the time he'd dropped her home. He'd stayed in her spare room and last night hadn't happened.

Any of it.

Toby retreated, had a cold shower to take his mind off last night and pulled on his rumpled clothes. By the time he joined Saskia in the kitchen again, she'd poured him a mug of coffee and had just sliced up the hot ciabatta bread. A butter dish—Saskia was the only person he knew who owned a butter dish, let alone used it, and insisted on very lightly salted proper butter instead of polyunsaturated margarine—sat in the middle of the table, together with a lead crystal bowl of strawberry preserve that she'd decanted from the jar.

She was definitely a woman who didn't compromise. On anything.

Ruefully, he slid onto a seat. 'This looks lovely.'

She shrugged. 'Breakfast. Help yourself.'

'Thanks.'

Eating did nothing to help the sick feeling in his stomach. Her face was carefully schooled and he couldn't read what she was feeling, what she was thinking. Somehow he had to persuade her to give them a chance. Had to speak first, before she—

Too late.

'Toby, we need to talk.'

Here it came.

'About last night. It shouldn't have happened. I think we were both…a little emotional.'

A little? He could feel a muscle flickering in his jaw. He'd been *that* close to telling her how he really felt about her. How much he loved her. How she made him complete.

But, afraid she'd push him away again if he said it in words, he'd chickened out and let his body say it for him. 'Uh-huh,' he said, trying to sound as neutral as he could.

'You're my best friend.'

'And you're mine.'

He had that vulnerable puppy-dog look about him again, Saskia thought. But she'd have to harden her heart this time. The longer she let this go on, the worse it would be for both of them. She sighed. 'Toby. You know I care about you. More than…' More than cared. Which was why she had to let him go. 'Well. I've been trying to find the right woman for you.'

'The right woman for me?'

Whoops. Put that way, maybe it did sound a little patronising. 'Come on, Toby. You're so wrapped up in the hospital and you hardly ever date. So I thought maybe I could help you find someone who can make you happy. Someone who deserves you.'

'Did it ever occur to you,' he enquired mildly, 'that I might already have someone in mind? Like *you?*'

'I, um…' Yes. He'd made that pretty clear last night. But she couldn't give him what he wanted. She was unlikely to have one child, let alone the half-dozen Toby wanted. And as for his thoughts about being a house-husband—how could he do it if she was completely dependent on him? If she hadn't had this wretched disease, maybe they could have made a go of it. She liked Toby, respected him.

Loved him—more than she'd ever loved anyone else that she could remember.

But the rheumatoid arthritis would get in the way of everything. That was why she had to let him go—to give him a chance to find someone who could fulfil his dreams. 'Toby, it's not going to happen. Last night was…' She stopped. No, it hadn't been a mistake. It was a nugget of pure joy that she'd store up and remember during the bleak times ahead. She stared into her coffee. 'Last night shouldn't have happened. I don't want to lose your friendship. So, for both our sakes, let's just pretend it never happened.'

. She waited a beat. No response.

Then she looked up.

For a brief second she saw the pain in his eyes. Sheer, gut-wrenching pain, as if she'd just ripped his heart in two.

But then she blinked, and wondered if she'd really seen it. Because he was still the same Toby. Not smiling, admittedly, but he didn't look as if she'd just punched a huge hole in the bottom of his world. He looked as if today were just another ordinary day.

'If that's what you want.' He stood up. 'I'd better be going.'

But…hadn't he said he was on a late? He'd hardly taken a bite out of his bread, and he hadn't finished his coffee. 'Toby, I—'

'I'll take your skirt to the dry cleaner's.' His voice was cool, neutral. Very un-Toby-like.

She shook her head. 'It's OK. I'll do it.'

He shrugged. 'As you please. See you later.'

Though, from the way he said it, it sounded as if he had no intention of seeing her later. Not until he'd wrapped himself in tight, tight armour plating. Guilt flooded through her. 'Maybe we can have coffee this afternoon?'

'Probably won't have time. I need to check on some of my patients, and then there's the Christmas roster to sort out.' He lifted one shoulder, grabbed his jacket—and then he was gone.

Saskia remained exactly where she was. She'd done the right thing, she knew that. She'd saved Toby from a lifetime of misery, a lifetime of having her as a burden.

So why did it make her feel so bad? Why did it make her feel as if she'd lost everything she held most dear?

Then a really nasty thought struck her. Toby was still her best friend—wasn't he?

She stayed at the table, not touching the cooling bread or her coffee. A single mouthful would have made her sick. She didn't think she'd ever be able to eat hot buttered bread with strawberry jam again: the taste and scent would always remind her of this. After a long, long time, she scraped her chair back, put the bread, butter and strawberry conserve in the bin, poured the coffee down the sink and filled a bowl with hot water. But when she turned the radio on, the first notes of the song made her turn her back to the cupboards and sink down into a sitting position. It was way, way too appropriate. 'Hallelujah', a real rip-your-heart-out song. This version was all the more poignant because it was by one of her favourite singers—and Toby had bought her the CD on the first day of its release. Slipped it onto her desk, giftwrapped with a big pink bow round it. She hadn't even needed to look at the label to know it had been from him.

She stared into the distance, her eyes unseeing, and sang along with the record. And on the last word of the song, for the second time in twelve hours, Saskia did something she never, ever did. She let a tear fall down her cheek. And it burned like acid.

# CHAPTER ELEVEN

'GROW up,' Saskia told herself. 'You're thirty-one. You're too old for this.' Checking her emails three times in the space of five minutes, just in case Toby had sent her a message...it was ridiculous. Apart from the fact it was the sort of thing teenagers did, this was her *best friend* she was obsessing about!

And, as of last night, her lover. A thrill ran down her spine.

And, as of this morning, her best friend and *not* her lover. At her own stipulation.

She shifted uncomfortably in her seat. What a mess. She'd had good reasons to call a halt, but she couldn't get Toby out of her mind. The feel of his hands against her skin. The feel of his mouth against her skin. The soft murmur of his voice. Nobody had ever, ever made her feel as alive as Toby had made her feel last night. Nobody had even come close to making her feel the way Toby made her felt.

*Marry me.*

She knew what she'd get out of it. A man who made her laugh, knew how her mind worked and whose body could push her right over the edge. A man she liked, a man she trusted more than anyone else in the world. A man who wasn't afraid to show he cared. A man who could make her feel like the queen of the universe.

Toby was perfect.

But what would he get out of the deal? Marriage to a woman who couldn't give him the children he wanted. A woman who'd need him to do more and more things for her as time went on. A useless burden.

He'd be doing all the giving, and she'd be doing all the taking.

No way could Saskia handle that. If she ever married—which she'd always thought highly unlikely—she wanted an equal relationship. A relationship where they both gave, both took. Maybe sometimes there would be an imbalance—she wasn't naïve enough to think that life would always be perfectly smooth—but the giving and taking would even out, over the years. If she married Toby, she'd have to take more and more and more, and would be able to give less and less and less. He was only human. Eventually, he'd start to resent her, and their marriage would just fall apart.

Which was why she couldn't say yes.

Then she thought about last night again, and her whole body craved his touch.

This really, really wasn't good. Why the hell had she let herself get that involved? Why had she been so self-indulgent? Why hadn't she done the sensible thing and sent him home—even before he'd kissed her?

She tried and failed to concentrate on the paperwork that followed her rounds. It was just another day. Just another ordinary day. So why couldn't she settle to anything?

Probably guilt, she acknowledged. Last night, Toby had shared everything with her. He'd put himself completely in her hands. This morning, she'd pushed him away and she hadn't given him a proper explanation.

She owed him the truth.

She glanced at her watch. She was due a break. With any luck, so was he. Quickly, she dialled his extension.

'Paediatrics, Staff Nurse speaking.'

Damn. He'd switched his phone through. Which meant

either he was on rounds or with a patient. 'Hello, it's Saskia Hayward from Maternity. Is Toby there, please?'

'He's with a patient. Do you want me to send his registrar up?'

'No, it's...personal. Can you ask him to ring me when he's free, please?'

'Of course.'

Except Toby didn't ring, and Saskia found herself more and more unable to settle. Maybe she needed a caffeine kick. She left her office and was about to tell Kerry that she'd be in the canteen if she was needed when Georgina came over to her.

'Saskia, got a minute?'

'Sure. Problems?'

'Mmm. I'm not happy about Ariadne, the mum I'm working with at the moment. She's very short of breath, she's started coughing and her blood pressure's dropped.'

'What about the baby?' Saskia asked.

'Bradycardic.' The baby's heartbeat was too low, which could be dangerous.

Saskia was thoughtful. 'It sounds as if she's in shock.' If the mum was in shock, she was probably losing blood from somewhere. The most likely reason was a placental abruption.

'I've just got a bad feeling about this.'

Saskia had learned very early on that an experienced midwife's instincts were usually spot on. 'Are you thinking amniotic fluid embolism?' she asked. This was a condition where amniotic fluid or foetal cells entered the mother's circulation and caused cardio-respiratory collapse. Shortness of breath and low blood pressure were two of the signs.

'Maybe.'

Amniotic fluid embolism was very rare, affecting one in between eight thousand and thirty thousand pregnancies, depending on which statistics you believed. 'I've never seen a case, only read about it in textbooks,' Saskia admitted. It was impossible to predict who'd be affected and nobody knew what caused it. But the kicker was that it carried a very high risk of maternal death. 'How about you?'

'Once, when I was training, but that was years ago.' Georgina looked worried.

If only Jim was there—he'd probably treated a case before. But he was still on sick leave. Saskia was the most senior doctor available, so she knew she had to deal with it.

She thought quickly. Amniotic fluid embolism had two stages. The first was when the pulmonary artery—the main blood vessel leading to the lungs—tightened. That led to pulmonary hypotension, meaning that the capillaries in the lungs and around the heart didn't get enough oxygen, and the left side of the heart failed. The mum then developed acute respiratory distress.

If she survived this phase, the second stage of the embolism meant that she'd have a massive haemorrhage and often go into DIC—disseminated intravascular coagulation—which interfered with the blood's ability to clot and meant the mum would lose even more blood.

From what Saskia could remember from the textbooks, fifty per cent of women who had an amniotic fluid embolism died within the first hour of their symptoms developing. Those who survived had permanent neurological problems and were very likely to develop pulmonary oedema and need intensive care.

The only good thing was that the baby had a seventy per cent chance of survival.

The next couple of hours could be very, very grim.

'Is her partner with her?' Saskia asked.

Georgina nodded.

'If it is amniotic fluid embolism, it's not going to be pleasant—we might need to get him out of the room quickly.'

'I'll explain the situation to him, if it gets that far,' Georgina said. 'Just hope that I'm making a mountain out of a molehill.'

Considering that Georgina had fifteen years' experience more than she did, Saskia doubted it.

Georgina introduced Saskia to Ariadne and her husband, Spiridon, then Saskia checked the monitor linked to the baby. The baby's heartbeat was less than a hundred and ten beats per minute—the bradycardia Georgina had mentioned earlier. If the heartbeat dropped to sixty beats a minute or less and stayed like that for three minutes or so, they'd lose the baby. They needed to get Ariadne stabilised, and fast.

Saskia put an oxygen mask over Ariadne's face. 'I'm giving you some oxygen to help make breathing easier for you,' she said, turning the flow up to maximum. 'Georgina, can you bleep the anaesthetist for me?'

'Sure,' the midwife replied.

'Ariadne, I'm going to put a needle in your hand now—your blood pressure's very low, so I may need to give you some fluids to bring your blood pressure up again, OK?'

Ariadne nodded tiredly, and Saskia inserted the IV line. Ariadne was showing all the signs of shock—though she didn't appear to be losing any blood that Saskia could see. That meant an internal bleed: possibly due to an abruption, where the placenta tore away from the uterus; a ruptured uterus; or an inverted uterus.

'I'm going to give you a scan, Ariadne, so I can rule out a couple of problems,' Saskia said.

'Is the baby all right?' Spiridon asked.

'For now. I may need to take Ariadne to Theatre for a Caesarean, though, if the baby goes into distress,' Saskia warned.

Thank God they were in the room with the portable scanner. Saskia bared Ariadne's abdomen, squeezed gel onto it and ran the head of the scanner over the gel. There were no signs of an abruption, no signs of a ruptured uterus, and Ariadne's uterus was in a completely normal position. Damn. It was looking more and more like a case of amniotic fluid embolus. If only Jim was here.

But he wasn't, so she'd have to deal with it.

'BP's dropping,' Georgina said quietly. 'Anaesthetist's on his way.'

'Right. We need to get fluids into her, fast,' Saskia said, equally quietly.

Though the fluids didn't seem to affect Ariadne's blood pressure. Saskia was just about to suggest using inotropes when the monitor pinged.

'She's arrested,' Saskia said. 'Crash team,' she yelled. Worse and worse, Ariadne's heart wasn't in an abnormal rhythm—the monitor was showing the straight line of asystole. Shocking her heart with a defibrillator wasn't an option, but they might be able to start external pacing if one of the midwives could get a cardiac specialist in pretty quickly. In the meantime, they'd have to keep going with CPR. 'Spiridon, I'm afraid I'm going to have to ask you to leave,' she said.

'But—'

'We'll do our best for her,' Saskia said. 'But, trust me, this is going to be too distressing for you to watch.'

Kerry came in. 'You called, Saskia?'

'Yes, can you show Spiridon to the relatives' room, please, and call a cardiac specialist pronto?'

Kerry nodded, and shepherded Spiridon out of the room. Saskia asked, 'Georgina, can you bag?'

'Yes.'

Saskia noted the time, gave Ariadne a precordial thump, then rechecked her carotid pulse. Nothing.

She tilted Ariadne's head back, lifted her chin and cleared her mouth. Georgina gave Ariadne two breaths. Saskia, ignoring the throb in her wrists, placed the heel of her hand over the lower third of Ariadne's sternum and counted fifteen compressions. They continued CPR, watching the monitor, but there was no change.

'How's the baby doing?' Saskia asked.

'Holding on—just.'

'We're going to need to do a section,' Saskia said. 'We need to get the baby out as fast as we can now. Just let us get Ariadne back first. Can someone get Toby from Paeds?'

But even after the cardiologist and anaesthetist arrived, there was nothing they could do for Ariadne.

'We need the baby out, fast,' Saskia said. 'I'm going to do a section here.' Her hands were hurting like hell from the CPR, but what else could she have done? Refused to help?

Though the result was the same. Ariadne hadn't made it.

Saskia was going to make damned sure the baby made it. She wasn't going to let Spiridon lose his wife *and* his baby this near Christmas. Losing a whole family was way, way too much.

OK. Focus. We're going to save that baby, she told herself. Hold the scalpel. You know exactly where to make the incision. Georgina's ready to give the pressure you need on the top of the fundus and...

She nearly fumbled the incision.

*Bloody* hands. Why wouldn't they work properly when she needed them?

She took a deep breath as the amniotic fluid gushed out, then carried on with the Caesarean section. Where the hell was Toby? She needed him—*now*.

'Pressure, please, Georgina,' she said.

Just as she delivered the baby, she was aware of the door

opening. Toby? 'Perfect timing,' she said. 'There's a little girl here who needs you to check her out.'

Except it wasn't Toby. It was Judy, his registrar. 'Toby's with a patient,' she explained.

Saskia nodded. 'We lost the mum. I think I managed to get this little one out in time—but I don't want to lose her, too.'

'Sure.'

By the time Saskia had cleaned up and covered Ariadne's lower body, ready for her husband to see her, Judy had finished checking the baby. 'I'd suggest SCBU—' the special care baby unit '—just so we can keep an eye on her, but the chances are she'll be fine. You got her out in time.'

'Yeah.'

Judy laid a hand on Saskia's arm. 'Are you OK?'

'Just hate losing any of my mums. Or my babies.'

'It's terrible,' Judy said, and gave her a hug. 'But don't blame yourself. We do what we can, but we can't make it right for everyone.'

'I know.' But it still hurt. She took a deep breath. 'I'd better break the news to her husband.'

'I'll take the baby to SCBU.'

Saskia nodded. 'I'll bring him up when he's ready.'

'Want me to be with you when you tell him?' Georgina asked.

'Thanks, but I'll be OK. Go get yourself a coffee and something sugary.'

'Hey. It's nobody's fault. Chances are, if Jim had been here, the result would've been the same,' Georgina warned.

'Uh-huh.' Saskia forced a smile to her face. 'Catch you later.'

Breaking bad news to relatives was something she really, really hated. When she walked out of the room, Spiridon was pacing up and down the corridor. He turned and saw her, then raced over to her. 'Ariadne?'

She took a deep breath. 'Let's go to my office,' she said.

'No.' His face crumpled. 'Oh, God, no. Not… She's my life. She can't be.'

'I'm very, very sorry. We did everything we could.' Saskia's throat felt clogged with tears.

'And the baby?'

'You have a little girl,' Saskia said softly, shepherding him into her office and closing the door. 'Spiridon, I'm so sorry. What happened is what we call an amniotic fluid embolus—that means some of the amniotic fluid or the baby's cells got into Ariadne's circulation, and it caused problems with Ariadne's breathing and her heart.'

'But—how did it happen?'

'We don't know how or why it happens. Some doctors think it's an allergic reaction.'

'And she's dead.' He buried his face in his hands. 'Oh, God. How am I going to carry on without her?'

'You'll do it. For your little girl's sake.'

He didn't seem to hear her. 'Her family will never forgive me. They always said we should have stayed in Greece—that I should have got a job there, not come over here, so far away from them. How am I going to tell them?'

'Do you have family here? Anyone you'd like me to call?'

He closed his eyes and shook his head. 'They're all in Greece.'

'A friend?'

'I…' He rubbed his hand across his eyes. 'I'm sorry. I can't take this in.'

'It's hard,' Saskia said gently. 'But if you'd like to see her, I can take you to her. And if you'd like to see your little girl, I can take you up to the special care unit.'

'Special care? Is she going to be all right?'

'It's just a precaution—the paediatrician wants us to keep a close eye on her for a day or so. I had to give Ariadne an emergency Caesarean section so we could get the baby out in time. But your daughter should be home well before Christmas.' Bitter-sweet. A time for giving, a time for the precious gift of life to be celebrated—but Spiridon had also lost the woman he loved.

'And it's a little girl?'

She nodded.

He took a shuddering intake of breath. 'Ariadne said she didn't mind what we had, as long as the baby was healthy, but I know she wanted a little girl.' His voice wobbled. 'I'll call her after her mother. And she'll be beautiful. Just like my Ariadne.'

'Would you like me to take you to your wife?' Saskia asked. 'And I can stay with you for as long as you like.'

'Would you?'

'Of course.'

She stayed with him while he sobbed at Ariadne's bedside, and when Spiridon had composed himself again, she took him up to SCBU and introduced him to his daughter and the nurse who was looking after her.

'She's beautiful. She's got her mother's looks.' He swallowed hard. 'My little Ariadne.' He looked at Saskia, his eyes anxious. 'She really will be all right?'

'As I said, she's in here just so we can keep an eye on her and make sure nothing nasty develops. But there's a good chance everything will be fine. And she's got you on her side.'

'She'll always have her daddy. Always,' he vowed.

Saskia breathed normally again. It could have gone one of two ways—either Spiridon would have blamed the baby for killing his wife, or he'd have fallen in love with his daughter and sworn to protect her from harm. Thank heaven, it had gone the right way. Ariadne would definitely have an over-protective father, but she'd always know she was loved.

'I'll leave you to get to know your daughter,' she said quietly. 'But if you have any questions, anything you need, just come and see me. I'll ask the hospital chaplain to pop up and see you, if you like.'

'Thank you.'

She nodded, and left the unit. She called the hospital chaplain and the mortuary, then started on her paperwork to list her requests for the post-mortem. The important thing about the post-mortem was that the pathologist should examine the lungs for the presence of amniotic squames—that would confirm the diagnosis of amniotic fluid embolus.

To her relief, nothing out of the ordinary happened during the rest of the day, but when she finished her shift she felt drained. Right now, she really, really needed a hug.

In normal circumstances, she would have called Toby. But how could she after this morning? She could still see the look in his eyes from that morning, that brief second when she'd realised she'd ripped his heart out—and she hated herself for it. How could she possibly go to him for comfort when she'd hurt him so much?

Maybe Lyd…but Lyd had enough on her plate, looking after Paul.

Besides, she owed Toby a proper explanation. She'd handled things really, really badly this morning. She leaned against her car door and rang him from her mobile phone. His line was engaged; he was probably doing something on the Internet.

Last night, he'd called a truce with chocolates. Maybe she ought to do the same. She drove to the nearest large supermarket and spent a while in the chocolate aisle, choosing one of every type of white chocolate they had. She thought about putting them in a bag that had a reindeer on the front with a nose that flashed—that sort of thing was right up Toby's street—but then he might get the wrong message. It wasn't a Christmas present. It was a truce. She found a fuchsia-pink bag to put them in instead, just to make the point.

She drove over to his house, parked her car and leaned on his doorbell.

It took him a while to answer. When he did, she was struck by how tired he looked, with a trace of stubble on his face and shadows under his eyes. Maybe his day had been just as bad as hers. Right now, she just wanted to put her arms around him, hold him and make him feel better.

But she didn't want to risk him taking it the wrong way. So she simply smiled, and handed him the bag.

'What's this?'

'I owe you an apology,' she said quietly, 'And an explanation. So this is...kind of...' She couldn't think of the right word. 'Truce?' she said finally.

# CHAPTER TWELVE

SASKIA had come to him. She was on his doorstep, asking for a truce. Just like he'd done to her yesterday.

Toby noticed the bag she held out to him was bright pink. Trust her to get something so girly. He opened it and his eyes widened in surprise. It was stuffed full of white chocolate. It looked as if she'd picked every different type she could find, too—a bar containing ground coffee beans, a bar with dried strawberries, a bar of Belgian white chocolate, white chocolate lollies shaped like reindeer, a Father Christmas and a star, a bag of white chocolate snowballs and even some white chocolate Christmas tree decorations. The stuff she didn't even *consider* to be chocolate, the stuff she knew he loved. Just like he'd bought her the stuff she loved but he hated.

'Last night in reverse,' he said softly. 'But why do I get the feeling you're not intending to stay with me tonight?'

'It's not because I don't want to.'

The quiet admission stunned him. Saskia *wanted* to stay with him?

She coughed. 'I don't want to pour my heart out on the doorstep, Tobe.'

'Oh. Sorry.' She got him so mixed up nowadays he couldn't even think straight. Hadn't realised where they were. Stupid. 'Um, come in. Coffee?'

'Love one.' Her face twisted. 'Look, this isn't last night all over again. It just *sounds* like it.'

'Maybe we're just predictable. Coffee, chocolate and chat. It's what best friends do, isn't it?' He hoped the phrase 'best friends' hadn't come out bitterly. He hadn't

136

meant it to sound bitter. He just wished things could be different between them. How they'd been last night, before she'd let her head rule her heart again. When she'd lain in his arms and looked into his eyes as they'd both fallen into paradise.

He switched on the kettle in an attempt to stop himself turning troglodyte. Grabbing her and carrying her upstairs over his shoulder might make him feel a lot better for a few minutes, but it wasn't going to solve their problems. 'How are your hands?' he asked.

'They've been better.' She sighed and sat down at his kitchen table. 'I've had the most unutterably bloody day, Tobe. I had a case I'd only ever seen in a textbook—amniotic fluid embolism. My first maternal death in three years. I had to do an emergency section after we lost the mum.'

So she'd come to him for comfort.

Either he'd spoken aloud or she'd read it on his face, because she shook her head. 'No. I mean, yes, a hug would be nice, but that's not why I'm here. I don't want to use you.' She took a deep breath. 'I've come to give you an explanation. To tell you why I said this morning that we can only ever be friends.'

Even though she'd admitted that she wanted to spend the night with him again. He didn't get it. If she wanted him and he wanted her, why couldn't they be together? What was the problem? He couldn't see one.

'Right now, Tobe, my life's a mess. I can't even think straight.' She sighed. 'I don't know what to do about my career. I know I have to do the decent thing and resign, but I can't handle the idea of giving up my job. I'm…I suppose I'm too much like my parents. I live for my job, just like they do.' She bit her lip. 'I'm flattered that you asked me to marry you.'

Flattered? Not the reaction he wanted. He wanted her to

be delighted. To fling her arms round him, have a smile as wide as the universe and tell him she wanted to marry him more than anything in the world.

'If I ever did get married, it would be to—'

To him? His heart leaped.

'Someone I like and respect and trust…and…'

The last word was a whisper, as if it had been ripped from her. He wasn't quite sure if he'd heard it correctly, but no way could he ask her to repeat it. She was too stubborn. But he was sure she'd said it.

*Love.*

He knew she liked, respected and trusted him. Was she admitting that she loved him?

To his surprise, her eyes were glittering. Saskia never cried. Last night her face had been wet, but he wasn't sure who the tears had belonged to. Probably him. Emotional overload from finally making love with her.

'But I can't get married. Ever.'

All his instincts told him to pull her into his arms and let the heat between them change her mind. Yet something in her voice stopped him. Sure, he could overcome the barriers between them physically, but as soon as they were apart again he knew she'd put the barriers straight back up. 'Why not?' he asked carefully, handing her a mug of coffee.

'You know I was an accident.' The words sounded thick, as if they choked her to say them. 'My parents never really wanted me. They handed me over to a succession of nannies—neither of them was prepared to compromise their career for the sake of their child. They never even took Christmas Eve off to take me to see Santa. I'm just like them. I can't handle the idea of giving up being a doctor. Not for anyone or anything. I love my job so much. It's… It's who I am.' She bit her lip. 'So what kind of mother would I make?'

'Better than you think,' Toby said. 'If you really didn't care about your future children, you wouldn't even be asking the question. You'd just take it for granted that you'd do what you wanted and the kids would fit around you.'

Just as her own parents had done with her.

She shook her head. 'I'm too tired to argue with you, Toby. I'm trying to explain—to tell you the truth.'

If he kept interrupting her, he'd never find out what was holding her back. 'OK. I'll shut up and listen. Well, I'll try, anyway,' he amended.

'Then there's Connie. My dad's sister. She's got rheumatoid arthritis.'

And Saskia was worrying that she'd pass it on to their children? 'There isn't a proven genetic link for RA.'

She glared at him. 'That's *not* what I was trying to say. What I'm saying is that I've seen what the disease has made her become. Before I got it myself, I thought Connie was making a bit of a fuss over nothing—that she was exaggerating, so everyone would do things for her and she could just sit back and enjoy the attention. But now I know what the pain's like—on a bad day, the way it drags you down and leaves you feeling just drained and miserable and unable to think clearly. Maybe she started out like me. I don't know.' She shook her head helplessly. 'Connie's always had RA, ever since I've known her. But, heaven help me, if the pain's going to turn me into her... I can't do that to you, Toby. I don't want to become a manipulative, selfish burden who's going to ruin your life.'

This time, Toby reacted on his gut feeling. He pulled her off her chair and onto his lap. 'Listen. There's no way you'll ever become a manipulative, selfish burden. I've known you for thirteen years and you've always been independent. Too independent really—you never let people close.'

Her jaw set but, to his relief she didn't wriggle off his

lap and reclaim her chair. 'That's not true. There's you and Lyd.'

'And how long did it take you to tell me that you had RA?' he pointed out. 'I'm guessing that you haven't told her yet.'

'Well—no,' Saskia admitted. 'She's got enough on her plate.'

Toby raised an eyebrow. 'If the tablets hadn't fallen out of your bag, you wouldn't have told me, would you?'

'Yes. Of course I would.'

'When?'

She sighed. 'Eventually. When I'd worked out how.'

'When you'd already come to a decision, you mean. I'm never entirely sure what's in your head, Saskia. I can guess, most of the time—but there are layers and layers I'll never be able to uncover.'

She grimaced. 'It's how I am.'

'I know, and I accept that. What I'm telling you is that it's OK to lean on people, Saskia. That's what friends are for. You help each other through the bad times.' He stroked her cheek. 'And you're going to need a lot of help coming to terms with the fact that you'll have to start doing things at a normal person's pace, instead of Super-Saskia's pace.'

'Toby, life with me isn't going to be easy.'

He chuckled. 'State the obvious, why don't you?'

'No, I mean it's going to be hard. Really hard. There will be days when I can't do things. Days when I'll have to rely on you. And it'll happen more and more and more as the years go on. I don't want that. I don't want to lose my independence, and I don't want to drag you down.'

'You won't be dragging me down.'

'You say that now. But what about in twenty years' time?' Her face was anguished. 'Twenty years, when I've become a miserable, whiny person like Connie and just demand things all the time?'

'You won't be like your aunt. You'll be yourself.'

She growled in frustration. 'You're not taking me seriously.'

'I am. I just think you're underestimating yourself.'

'OK. Let's take it from another angle. You want a family. A big family, like the one you never had when you were a child. And don't deny it, Toby. I know you do.'

He sighed. 'Yes. I do.'

'I can't give you children. Not unless I stop taking the anti-rheumatic drugs—and I'm frightened of what that might do to me.' She swallowed hard. 'It scares me how much I might have to depend on you, without the drugs. It scares me spitless.'

Did she really think he'd let her down? Ever? 'I'll be there. You know that.'

'So we're back to the burden argument. Even if you don't think I'm a burden, *I'll* think I'm a burden. And I'll be as crabby as hell because I don't want to be like that.'

'There are other options, you know. If we want a family we could always become foster-parents or adopt children. That way, you wouldn't have to stop taking the anti-rheumatics but we'd still have children.'

'You've got an answer for everything.'

If it meant he could spend the rest of his life with her, the way he wanted to, of course he had. 'If we're being completely honest with each other now, can you cope with the bottom line?'

She was silent for a moment. Then she nodded. 'All right. Tell me.'

Too late to back out now, even though his head was yelling at him not to be a fool, to back off before he lost her for good. His heart was hammering so hard, he was sure she must be able to feel it. And his mouth felt as if someone had just filled it with sand—he couldn't even swallow. 'I want you,' he said quietly. 'I've wanted you for years—probably since the first day I met you.' It was out now. And she didn't look that shocked. He took courage from it. 'Why do you think I hardly ever dated? Nobody ever matched up to you.'

'But…' Her face coloured. 'Don't tell me last night was just natural talent?'

He grinned. So she *had* been affected by what had happened between them. It had been the best sex she'd ever had, too. 'Not all. Some of it was practice.' At her narrowed eyes, his grin broadened. If she was jealous—and she certainly *looked* jealous—then they stood a chance. 'I'm a man, Saskia. I have needs and I can't always deny them.' He sobered again. 'But, as I said, nobody ever matched up to you, and I made it clear I wasn't in the market for a relationship. I didn't meet anyone else I wanted to be with for the rest of my life.'

'Don't put me on a pedestal,' she warned. 'I'm not perfect.'

He stroked her face. 'I know. You're clever, you're a brilliant doctor, you're great company and you're beautiful—and you're outspoken, opinionated and completely impossible. Oh, and you're rubbish at telling jokes.' He smiled. 'I don't want perfect. I want you.'

She had no answer to that.

Toby figured they'd already reached the point of no return. So he may as well tell her the rest of it. 'I love you, Saskia. I love you for who and what you are. Nothing's ever going to change that.' He waited a beat. 'And I think you love me, too.'

'Toby—'

'You've said it before. Yes, I know you meant you love me as a friend, but it's more than that between us and you know it. So you're running scared. You've gone into denial—you wanted to prove to yourself as well as to the world that you weren't in love with me. That's why you had so many dates. And they weren't what you wanted, so most of them didn't even get a second date, let alone anything more.'

She scowled. 'Since when did you do a psychology rotation?'

'And that's a defensive reaction.'

Her scowl deepened. 'Sometimes I could murder you.'

'I'm telling you the truth,' he said inexorably. 'Are you going to admit it?'

She sighed. 'I didn't sleep around.'

'I know.'

'I'm picky. There weren't many men who made it that far.'

'I know. Though it wouldn't matter to me if they had. I'm not interested in them. I want you.' He was also pretty certain that he was the only man who'd ever spent the whole night in Saskia's bed, skin to skin. And he'd done it twice: once at Lydia's and once at Saskia's. Which made him very sure of his ground. 'You just have to be brave, Saskia. Take the last step. Just one little word, that's all. Will you marry me?'

One little word. It would be so easy. She wanted to say it. She *ached* to say it. But how could she?

Toby had really got under her skin. He'd made her face something she hadn't really thought about before: the reason why she'd dated so many men and refused most of them a third date, let alone anything else. She'd been running a mile from the fact that she'd met the man she wanted to spend the rest of her life with, and that choosing him might mean making other choices, choices she hadn't been ready even to think about.

She still wasn't ready to think about them.

'I...need time,' she said.

His face closed. 'I see.'

'I'm not rejecting you. Not outright.' Oh, hell, how could she do this without hurting him? 'I just need to sort things in my head, Toby.' There was one person she needed to talk to: one person who might help her understand. If she could get leave, maybe they could have a heart-to-heart. 'I need some space to think.'

'OK. I'm not going to push you into anything you don't want.' He swallowed. 'But if you decide you want me, you'll have to come to me.'

She nodded. 'That's fair. I've already put you through the mill. Heaven help me, I don't want to hurt you, Toby. I just can't see my way through this right now.' She leaned her head against him briefly. 'And that's why I'm not going to stay here tonight. I want you—and…and, I think you're right.'

'About?'

Why couldn't she say it? Why couldn't she just back down and admit that she loved him, too, that she wanted to spend the rest of her life with him and to hell with her RA?

Because, unless she was sure they were going into this as equals, that she could give as much as she took, she couldn't do it.

'I…' She closed her eyes. 'Don't push me, Toby.'

He leaned his forehead against her hair. 'I'm sorry. I just wanted to hear you say it.'

She wanted to say it, too. But she had a mountain to climb first. 'Until everything's clear in my head, I can't. I can't promise you anything.'

'OK.' He held her close. 'No pressure. I'm not going to ask you again.'

She nodded, and wriggled out of his embrace. 'As soon as I've handed the department back to Jim, I'll ask him if I can have some time off. If he says yes, I'll be away for a few days so, um, I might not be in touch. I need to get my head straight.'

He folded his arms. 'You know where I am.'

And how easy it would be to run to him. But she wouldn't do it, until she was sure it was the right thing—for both of them.

'I'll, um, catch you later. I'll see myself out.' But she wasn't going to kiss him goodbye. She didn't think she and Toby would ever do friendly kisses again. She couldn't trust herself. The moment they touched each other, the kiss would turn to desire. And that wasn't fair on either of them.

# CHAPTER THIRTEEN

Saskia slept badly that night, and woke wishing that she'd given in to her instinct and spent the night in Toby's arms. She probably wouldn't have got any more sleep, but at least she would have woken up with a smile on her face.

And then she'd have hated herself for using Toby.

She dragged herself out of bed, and was at the hospital early enough to decorate Jim's office and the staffroom with Welcome Back banners hanging from all the tinsel before the consultant walked into the department.

'Wow. Proper coffee, Christmas florentines and mince pies. Do I take it that you missed me, or are you trying to prepare me for the handover from hell?' he asked Saskia with a grin.

'We all missed you,' Georgina said. 'Even though our Saskia managed to fill your shoes very well.'

'Just doing my job,' Saskia said with a shrug.

'No, doing *mine*,' Jim said, smiling at her.

'But you're back now, and I'm happy to hand the reins back. No lifting, though,' Saskia warned. 'You make one of us do it, not you, OK?'

'Ah, how I missed your bossiness,' he said, laughing. 'Go on, then. Hit me with the handover.'

He took a plate of florentines; they went into his office and he grinned as he saw how Saskia had decorated his office. 'Ah, it's good to be back. It wouldn't be Christmas without my reindeer lights.'

'Or without you as our ward Santa. Though you'll need an elf or two to carry the presents round for you.' She winked at him, then took him through what had happened

146

in his absence. 'I really could have done with you being around yesterday. We had a mum with amniotic fluid embolism.'

He looked serious. 'That's rare. And usually...'

She nodded. 'Yeah. I lost her.'

'Don't you dare blame yourself, Saskia.'

'Losing a mum is always bad, but this time of year...it's worse. It makes the tinsel look garish. How can you tell someone they've lost someone they love, when they can hear "Joy to the World" being sung everywhere?' She sighed. 'I thought afterwards maybe I should have phoned you for advice, asked you to come back a bit early.'

'But by the time I got here, it would have been too late anyway. And my guess is that you did everything I would have done. Don't doubt yourself.' He paused. 'How's the baby?'

'I nipped into SCBU this morning before my shift. Little Ariadne's doing well. She'll be going home in a couple of days.'

He smiled. 'Good. You did well.'

'Mmm.' This was the opening she needed. 'Jim...I know it's awkward timing, with people wanting days off for last-minute Christmas shopping and what have you, but I need a few days off. Like, um, from tomorrow.'

'Is everything all right?'

Jim was her colleague. Her boss. And he sounded more concerned about her than her parents ever had. Saskia could have howled. 'I just have a few things to think about. I'll, um, need to have a chat with you when I get back.'

He frowned. 'This sounds serious.'

She nodded. 'It is.'

'Anything you want to talk about right now?'

'No. I need to do some thinking first.'

'Fine. Take however long you need—I'll get a locum in. I'll be here if you need to discuss anything. But...' he lifted one hand to stop her speaking '...let me say now you're the best registrar I've ever had and, as far as I'm concerned, you have a great future in obstetrics.'

'Thanks, Jim.' Though she could hardly force the words out. It's not bloody fair, Saskia thought. Three months ago she'd have been delighted by Jim's praise. The best Christmas present she could have asked for. Now it just depressed her. Obstetrics was what she wanted to do, but she knew her body just wasn't going to let her do it.

At least her shift was relatively quiet. After she came off duty, she put an auto-respond on her email, saying that she was away and referring all professional queries to Jim. She resisted the urge to phone or email Toby—until she'd got things clear in her head, it wasn't fair to mess him about.

When she got home, she made what she thought might be the most important phone call of her life. Though, once the arrangements were made, she couldn't settle to any-thing—she just wandered aimlessly through her flat. She flicked through the TV channels: nothing she wanted to watch. No music she wanted to listen to. No book she could lose herself in. She couldn't even concentrate on work, or mess about on the Internet, or do one of the logic problems that usually diverted her. And it was a long, long time be-fore she managed to fall asleep.

The next morning, on her way down to Sussex, Saskia took a detour to the little Peak District village where Lydia lived. Toby was right. She'd already put this off too long. It was time to come clean.

'It'll Be Lonely This Christmas' was playing on the ra-dio. Too close to the truth for comfort—and it'd be for more than just Christmas, too. It'd be for life. Curling her lip, Saskia switched stations. Christmas carols—she wasn't in the mood for them, either. She flicked to a commercial station, and it was another song of Christmas love and loss.

And it was only early December. By Christmas Eve, everyone would be thoroughly sick of Christmas songs, she thought grumpily.

'Hello! I didn't know you were off today.' Lydia welcomed her with a hug. 'Come in. Paul's having a rest, Billy's at nursery and Helena's snoring her head off. Ignore the mess—Billy insisted on starting his picture of Father Christmas made out of tissue-paper balls before breakfast, and I haven't had time to tidy up yet. Coffee?'

'Yeah. Please.'

'Everything all right? You look a bit down.'

Saskia grimaced. 'Bad week. Lost a mum the other day. Amniotic fluid embolism.'

Lydia pursed her lips. 'Nasty. But don't blame yourself.'

'That's what Jim said. And Toby.'

'They're both senior to you, so listen to them.' Lydia made the coffee while Saskia sat at the kitchen table and crumbled a *lebkuchen* onto a plate.

'OK. Spit it out. What's *really* wrong?' Lydia asked.

'How do you mean?'

Lydia pointed to Saskia's plate. 'That's *lebkuchen*. German Christmas gingerbread, and you love the stuff. If you're playing with it, not eating it, something's up.'

Saskia sighed. 'OK. Um, there isn't an easy way to tell you, so I'll do it straight. I've got rheumatoid arthritis.'

'Oh, Saskia.' Lydia put her arms round Saskia and held her close. 'That's tough. When did you find out?'

'Um, nearly three months ago.'

'So the tablets are starting to work?'

Saskia shook her head. 'Not yet. Not noticeably.' And it scared her that they wouldn't. That she'd have to change her medication to something stronger—leaving her fewer and fewer choices in reserve for when things got really bad.

'Why didn't you tell me before?'

The question she'd been dreading. Though Lydia, at

least, didn't sound quite as hurt and accusatory as Toby had. 'I had to come to terms with it myself first. And then Paul had his operation—you had enough on your plate. And now it's the run-up to Christmas and I didn't want to put a dampener on things.'

'Saskia, you're my best friend. I've always got room for you—you know that.'

Saskia wriggled uncomfortably. 'I'm not very good at sharing.'

'Just bossing people about. Yeah. We know. So. Have you told work?'

'Not yet.' Saskia sighed. 'I need to decide what I'm going to do. It's going to get to the point where I can't do obstetric surgery, so I'm not going to be any use in the department.'

'How about retraining as a GP?' Lydia suggested.

'It's not me, Lyd—don't get me wrong, I'm not having a go at your choice of career. I just like working in a hospital. I like being right in the middle of a big, noisy place.' Feeling that she belonged. She'd never felt that with her parents—the hospital was her family.

Lydia nodded. 'Maybe there's another speciality you could retrain in.'

Just what Toby had suggested. 'But what? I love the maternity ward. Even when we were doing our house officer year, I knew that was where I wanted to be. Nowhere else comes even close. There was never any other choice. I'm an obstetrician, Lyd. It's *who* I am as well as what I am.'

Lydia reached over and took her hand. 'Oh, Saskia. I wish I could wave a magic wand for you.'

'They don't exist.' Saskia shrugged. 'I just need to have some time away. Time to think. I'm probably going to retrain as a lawyer.'

'What? But…you love medicine.'

'I love being an obstetrician,' Saskia corrected. 'Which I can't be any more. And I don't think I can handle working in another department. I can't do something that I feel's second-best.'

'Have you told Toby?'

Saskia nodded. 'The night we took Billy swimming. I dropped my bags and he found the methotrexate.'

'Ouch.' Lydia looked sympathetic. 'Did he give you a hard time about it?'

'Yeah. Then he, um, asked me to marry him.'

Lydia didn't seem the remotest bit surprised. 'Are you going to?'

'How can I?'

Lydia spread her hands. 'Because you're in love with him, you stupid woman.'

Saskia frowned. 'That's what he said. Have you been discussing it with him?'

'No. I just know you better than anyone else does—except maybe Toby. Saskia, I've said it before: you're made for each other.'

Saskia shook her head.

'You *are*,' Lydia insisted. 'But your childhood's made you panic about the marriage and family bit.' She smiled wryly. 'For someone who got the best exam results in our year, you can be remarkably dense. Of course you're not going to follow your parents' pattern. Look at your first reaction when Paul was taken ill in Canada! You came straight over and told me you'd stand in for me if I wanted to go over to Vancouver.'

'Not just me. Toby, too.'

'Yes. That's what *family* does. And Billy's been telling me what a brilliant time he had, how you made snowflake decorations and helped him make a Christmas card for me and Paul, how it was almost like having another mum and dad. Then look at the way you are with the kids anyway.

You take Billy to music classes when you can, and you spoil him rotten with books and art stuff—but, best of all, you give both of them your time. You read stories to them. You sing to Helena—and don't deny it, I've heard you. You draw things with Billy. Half the time you're here you spend on the floor playing with the kids. So don't say you're like your parents. You're not.'

Saskia laced her fingers together, willing the twinges of pain to go away. 'It scares me, Lyd. I don't want to end up like Connie.'

'Your aunt?'

Saskia nodded. 'I'm going to see her. Spend a couple of days with her.'

'Good idea. Maybe you'll realise then that you won't turn into her. You'll always be you.'

'Will I?'

'Yes. Trust me. I'm a doctor.'

Despite herself, Saskia smiled.

'That's better,' Lydia said.

'I actually found myself crying the other day. Me. Super-Saskia. The woman who copes with everything and never, ever cries,' Saskia admitted.

'Idiot. Apart from anything else, depression often goes with RA. Next time you feel even the slightest bit low, ring me. I'll come over with the tissues and the chocolate. You know, keeping things like this to yourself doesn't make you stronger. It makes you feel lost.'

'How did you get to be so wise?'

'I've seen it in dozens of patients. The strong, silent, stubborn ones are always the ones things hit hardest.' Lydia hugged her. 'So don't do it again. That's what I'm here for: to share the bad times as well as the good. You've been there for me. Let me be here for you.'

'Thanks.' Saskia gave her a wobbly smile. 'And I'm sorry I'm so bad at this.'

Lydia grinned. 'Hey, it's done my ego a power of good to find out that you're not completely invincible!'

'Oh, ha.' Saskia glowered at her, and took a *lebkuchen*. This time she ate it.

'It'll do you good to have some time away. Think about what you want from life. Look, as one door closes, another one always opens. And don't you call me Pollyanna either,' Lydia said sharply, as if reading the look on Saskia's face. 'It's true. Right now, you've lost your focus. But over the next few days something will turn up. Something good.'

'You mean, I'll agree to marry Toby?'

'No, though that's a good idea as well. He's been in love with you for ever. And I reckon you feel the same way. That's why—'

Saskia groaned, cutting her off. 'Are you quite sure you haven't discussed this with Tobe? It's exactly what he said. I had strings of men because I was scared to face up to my feelings for him.'

'We haven't discussed it,' Lydia said, 'but he's right on the money. You'd be good together. I've always said that. Now, go and see Connie. Think about what *you* want to do. No ifs, no buts: just what you really want to do.'

'Yeah. I will.' Saskia pushed her chair back. 'I'll see you when I get back.'

'All right. Have a safe journey. And text me when you get there so I know you've arrived safely.'

Her best friend cared that much, whereas her parents never had. They'd always remained detached, just assumed that everything was all right unless they heard otherwise. Saskia's throat tightened. 'Yeah. I will.'

Saskia drove down to Sussex in a slightly happier frame of mind. She stopped at a large supermarket on the edge of the seaside town where Connie lived and bought a bright pink azalea and a large box of chocolates, then parked in the visitors' area outside Connie's flat.

She couldn't remember the last time she'd seen her aunt. All she could really remember was a woman old before her time, who always dressed in severe black, never wore make-up—not even a smear of lip colour—and whose mouth had deep downward grooves on either side.

Part of Saskia didn't want to be here. Didn't want to see what she could turn into. But she needed some answers, and Connie was the only one who could give them to her.

Putting off the moment for a few seconds more, Saskia sent a text to Lydia to let her know she'd arrived safely, then pressed the button on the intercom.

Connie buzzed her niece into the flat, but didn't bother rising from the sofa.

'Hello, Aunt Connie.' Saskia kissed her cheek. Connie's skin felt thin and papery. She looked the same as Saskia remembered—old, thin and lined, dressed in black, hunched over. 'I brought you a plant.'

'Oh. Thank you.'

Saskia had never heard such insincere words. 'I thought that way you'd be able to enjoy the flowers without having to worry about lifting the vase to change the water,' she said, trying to sound bright and breezy and cheerful.

'Yes.'

Lord, Lord, Lord. Please don't let me get like that, Saskia thought. Monosyllabic, uninterested in anything… Why on earth had she come here? This was turning out to be a huge mistake.

'Um, shall I put it on a saucer for you?'

'If you like.'

So listless. Not caring what happened. Or maybe, Saskia thought with a pang of guilt, Connie saw people so rarely now that she didn't know how to socialise with people any more. If they could barely even manage polite conversation, how on earth was she going to be able to talk to Connie about something as awkward as her medical condition?

It had been so much easier on the phone. Or maybe she'd been less ill at ease then, and Connie was simply reacting to her niece's behaviour.

Clearly Connie wasn't going to offer her a drink. She decided to take matters into her own hands. If it killed her, she was going to get Connie to talk to her. 'Shall I make us both a coffee?' she asked.

'If you want.'

Saskia busied herself in Connie's kitchen, even though she really wanted just to run. To run as far as possible from here, from what she might become.

'I was surprised when you called,' Connie said, when Saskia brought a tray of coffee in.

A deserved rebuke, Saskia knew. 'I haven't been good at staying in touch. I'm sorry.'

'I expect you're busy, being a doctor.'

Here it came: the descent into self-pity. Me, me, me, me, me. Well, not this time, Saskia thought. This time Connie was going to think about someone else. 'Not for much longer,' she said coolly.

Connie frowned. 'Why?'

'I've got rheumatoid arthritis. I won't be able to hold a scalpel properly or do half the procedures I need to do.'

'Oh, my dear.' Connie's eyes filled with tears. 'I'm so sorry.'

'It happens. I've just got to come to terms with it.' Saskia bit her lip. 'Aunt Connie, can I ask you something personal?'

'Well, if you...?' Connie's voice tailed off, and she mopped at her eyes.

No. You are *not* going to pull a guilt trip on me now, turn the conversation back round to yourself and how you feel, Saskia thought. I need to know things. 'What did you do, before you had RA?'

Connie stared at her. 'Before?'

Connie *must* have done something…mustn't she? 'Your job?' Saskia tried.

There was a long, long silence. But Saskia, as a doctor, was used to waiting, and was sure the same principle would apply here. Give Connie space and she'd give Saskia more information.

Eventually, Connie said tonelessly, 'I was a florist. I had my own shop.'

Saskia couldn't imagine it. 'Why did you give it up?'

'Same as you. My hands wouldn't work properly.' Connie wrapped her arms around herself, as if protecting herself against old hurts. 'I won trophies for my flower arranging. But I couldn't do it any more. I couldn't hold the secateurs properly, couldn't cut woody stems, fumbled halfway through arrangements and ruined them.'

'Couldn't you have still run the shop without doing the flowers?'

Connie shook her head. 'What was the point? It was the flowers I loved.'

No wonder she'd reacted so badly to the pot plant. It had been a reminder of everything she'd lost. Just as every baby Saskia would pass in the street in future would be another reminder of the career she'd loved so much and lost. 'I'm so sorry. I never knew,' Saskia said softly.

'Why should you? I know what the family thinks of me, Saskia. I'm a whining old bag—give me an inch and I'll demand a few miles.'

Saskia flushed. It was true. What could she say? 'Um.'

'And I put things on, make a huge fuss to get attention.'

'I know what the pain's like now,' Saskia said. 'So, no, I don't think you were putting it on.'

'Maybe I was,' Connie said.

Saskia stared at her. 'What?'

'I was lonely. I thought people might come and see me more often if they thought I couldn't cope, if I needed them.' Connie sighed. 'But it backfired on me. It pushed them away, because they couldn't stand me clinging. Didn't want the burden.'

There was nothing Saskia could say without sounding rude or feeling as if she were rubbing salt in Connie's wounds.

'You won't make that mistake,' Connie said.

'Maybe not. But I've done my fair share of pushing people away,' Saskia admitted.

'I did that, too, when I found out what rheumatoid arthritis was going to mean for me.' Connie said. 'I let Hugh go.'

'Hugh?'

'Hugh Pickering. My fiancé. We'd set a date for the wedding, started planning everything. Your father was going to be our best man.' Connie grimaced. 'And then I was diagnosed with *this*. What use would I be as a wife, a cripple? And then they told me I couldn't have children, not unless I stopped the drugs—which would make my condition worse. I couldn't do that to him, make him give up his whole future because he'd have to care for me.'

Saskia's thoughts exactly.

Connie shrugged. 'I imagine things are different now.'

Saskia swallowed. 'No, it's the same,' she whispered.

'And the man you pushed away?'

Was it that obvious? 'I've known him for years. He's my best friend. Except…suddenly things changed. But he wants a big family. I can't give that to him.' She swallowed hard. 'You know. You did the same.'

'If I had my time over again,' Connie said, 'it'd be different. I'd have given Hugh the choice instead of breaking our engagement without telling him why. Does your young man know about the arthritis?'

Saskia nodded.

'And?'

'He says it doesn't change anything.'

'Then you have a choice,' Connie said. 'You can be together. Enjoy your time. Or you can push him away and end up lonely, like me. Making people feel guilty to force them into coming to see you and stop you feeling so alone…except then they start avoiding you because they hate the guilt. So you feel even more lonely. And the second anyone pays you attention, you're so hungry for it that you want more and more and more—and it scares people away. It's a vicious circle, and even if you want to break it, you can't.'

'Oh, Connie.' Saskia shifted to sit on the sofa next to her aunt and, for the first time she could ever remember doing so, put her arms round the older woman. 'I'm sorry. I never realised.'

'Why would you? You're young. And you know what your parents are like.'

'Yeah. Work, work and more work. I was heading that way myself. Living for the hospital.'

'What will you do now?'

'I don't know,' Saskia said honestly. 'I can't stay on as a doctor. I'd be putting my patients at risk, and that isn't fair. My boss told me yesterday that I had a great future. If only he knew.'

'You still have a future,' Connie said. 'You just need to find something else you can do—something where it doesn't matter if your hands knot up. Maybe you could be one of those radio doctors or something.'

'Right now, I can't see past anything other than the fact I can't work in the maternity unit any more,' Saskia admitted.

'Give yourself time. But don't give up on yourself. I should never have given up the shop—even if I couldn't do flowers any more, I could still have taught others to do it, got the pleasure through seeing them develop. I could have taken on a partner, to take the pressure off me on the days when I didn't feel up to things.' Pain and regret flickered over Connie's face. 'No, if I had my time over again, I'd be different.'

'You could be different now,' Saskia said.

She shook her head. 'I'm too old, too set in my ways. But you're young. Give yourself a chance. Give your young man a chance, too.'

Maybe, just maybe, she would.

'Don't let yourself be lonely, Saskia. It'll crush you far more than the pain in your joints.'

Lonely. Just like Connie was now. Saskia's heart twisted. 'I've booked into a hotel,' she said. 'On the seafront. Maybe…while I'm here, maybe you'd like to come and have dinner with me? I can pick you up.'

'I can't remember the last time I went out to dinner,' Connie said.

'Take your own advice. Give yourself a chance,' Saskia said.

'Maybe,' Connie said, 'just maybe, you're right.'

# CHAPTER FOURTEEN

SASKIA spent the next few days in Sussex, getting to know her aunt. Connie was very quiet over dinner the first night, but gradually relaxed with Saskia, to the point where Saskia managed to persuade her to join the town horticultural society. 'Connie, you like flowers and plants. OK, so you can't arrange them yourself any more and you can't do the weeding and hoeing and what have you, but you can get someone to help you. Why cut yourself off from something you enjoy?'

'It's a Hayward thing,' Connie said grimly. 'All or nothing.'

Saskia could understand that. She saw it in her father; she could see it in herself, too. 'Sometimes you have to learn to compromise.'

'Easier to say it than do it,' Connie said.

A truth that hit home. Uncomfortably so. When had Saskia ever compromised? But she was going to have to learn to do it now. 'OK. Here's the deal. I'll try if you will,' Saskia suggested.

Connie laughed. 'I wish I'd known you were like this. I thought you were like Marcus.'

'Efficient and clinical?' Saskia guessed wryly. 'I suppose I am.'

'No. You've got a good heart. Don't neglect it.'

Saskia started her last morning in Sussex with a pre-breakfast walk along the beach—a perfect December day, when the air was crisp and the sky was pale blue and the surf rushed over the pebbled shoreline. She'd forgotten her

160

gloves, so she shoved her hands in her pockets to keep them warm—she'd already learned the hard way that letting her hands get cold meant they hurt a lot later.

She still had no idea what she was going to do about her job. But Toby... She knew exactly what she was going to do. And it wasn't something she could do on the phone. She needed to see him—as soon as possible.

She packed before breakfast, checked out straight afterwards, then called in to say goodbye to Connie before she set out for home.

She'd just finished unpacking when her doorbell rang. She glanced at her watch and frowned. She wasn't expecting visitors. Nobody knew she was back yet, and it was a weird time for anyone to call by on the off chance. She hadn't let Toby or Lyd know she was on her way back, and Toby would be at work anyway at this time of day. A delivery of some sort maybe?

When she checked through the spyhole before opening the door, she blinked hard in surprise. The very last person she'd expected.

She opened the door and stood aside. 'Hello, Mother.'

'Hello, Saskia.' Antonia Hayward breezed in.

'I wasn't expecting you.'

'I know.'

Her mother had been to Sheffield twice in all the years Saskia had lived there. She couldn't hold back the question. 'What are you doing here?'

Antonia shrugged. 'You hung up on your father. You didn't return our calls or our emails.'

Saskia returned the shrug. 'I've been away.'

'I know.'

Saskia narrowed her eyes. 'Connie told you?'

'She said you'd been to see her.'

'Yes. She's very lonely.'

'Hardly surprising. You know what she's like.'

Saskia felt her jaw tighten. 'Do you have any idea what it's like, not being able to do the things you love—to feel helpless all the time?'

'No, but I do know one thing. You can only help people if they're prepared to help themselves, too.' Antonia sighed. 'I tried with Connie but...she just didn't want to know.'

'Maybe you offered the wrong sort of help.' Saskia folded her arms. Right now, she wasn't in the mood for dealing with her mother. But years of conditioning meant she had to ask the question, even though she didn't particularly want to. 'Have you eaten?'

'I had a sandwich on the train.'

'Would you like some coffee?'

'Thank you.'

Antonia followed Saskia into the kitchen. For a moment Saskia considered giving her mother instant coffee and long-life milk, then she remembered she didn't have any and banged the cafetière onto the worktop.

'When did Connie ring you?' she asked.

'Just after you left this morning.'

So what was her mother doing here now? Unless... She sighed. 'Obviously she told you the rest of it, too. I've got rheumatoid arthritis. Like her.'

Antonia smiled. 'Don't be so dramatic. You're nothing like Connie.'

'Actually, Mother, I think I am.' Now she'd got to know Connie a bit better, Saskia could see a lot of common ground between them.

'Rubbish. You'll cope with your condition.'

Her mother really had no idea. Saskia shook her head. 'I can't be a doctor any more. I can't do my job properly.'

'No, I can see you don't want to put the hospital at risk of a malpractice suit,' Antonia mused, sitting down at the table and accepting the mug of black coffee Saskia handed her.

Oh, typical. Antonia saw everything in terms of the law. Saskia sat opposite her mother. 'No, Mother, you don't understand. It's the *patients* I care about, not administration. I'm supposed to treat people, not hurt them!'

'So you've decided to retrain. Fair enough. Better to do something than be idle.' Antonia nodded. 'But you're not cut out to be a lawyer. Your father thinks the same.'

'You've been discussing me?'

'Don't look so surprised.'

'But…you never talk.'

Antonia scoffed. 'Of course we do.'

When? 'I thought you led separate lives.'

'We don't work together, but we have lunch together most days. If he's not held up in court and I'm not stuck in a client meeting, that is.'

Saskia had had no idea.

Antonia rolled her eyes. 'Saskia, we've been married for thirty-five years. Do you really think we'd still be married if we didn't want to be together?'

'I… It's just you never seemed to spend any time together when I lived at home.'

'If you want to get to the top in your career, you have to work at it. You know that. Look at you, acting consultant at your age.' Was that maternal pride Saskia heard in Antonia's voice? 'You're like me—you've always been focused.'

Saskia shook her head. 'I'm not like you. I care about people.'

'I care.'

'Really?' Saskia's temper snapped. 'I've never seen the evidence. I've never seen you and my father hold hands or even kiss.'

'Just because we're not demonstrative in public, it

doesn't mean we don't love each other. We understand each other, Saskia. We complete each other.'

'Maybe. But there wasn't room for me,' Saskia said quietly.

'You're our daughter. Our one and only.'

'I was an accident.'

Antonia frowned. 'Since when?'

'I overheard Connie talking to you one night. When I was small, and you thought I was asleep.'

Antonia sighed. 'You know what Connie's like. She'll do anything to get attention. Stirs things up.'

'No. She's just made some wrong choices and wasn't very good at trying to change things when she realised she'd got it wrong.'

To Saskia's surprise, Antonia didn't argue. She took her daughter's hands across the table. 'Listen to me, Saskia. You weren't an accident. The thing is, in my day there weren't such things as career breaks. I'd worked hard to get where I had—like you, I always knew what I wanted to do, right from when I was small. If my boss had thought I was desperate to start a family, my career would have stopped right there. So, yes, I admit that we made out that you were an accident. We had to, for the sake of my job. But, believe me, you were planned.'

Saskia couldn't quite believe what she was hearing. All her life she'd thought she'd been a mistake. And now her mother was telling her that she wasn't?

'I wasn't a stay-at-home mother, and I'm sorry if you felt you missed out. But if I'd stayed at home with you, that would have been an end to my career—and I'd have resented you for it. I'd have resented every single second I spent with you.' Antonia shook her head. 'I didn't want that. The way I planned it, I'd have everything—my career *and* my child.'

Saskia didn't buy that. Career, yes; child, no. 'You left

me with the nanny most of the time. I can't even remember
going to the park with you at the weekend.'

'I tried, a couple of times. I discovered I wasn't very
good at that sort of thing, so I thought you'd be better off
with someone who knew what they were doing.' Antonia
sighed. 'Being your mother was the first thing I'd ever
failed at. I just wanted to be a good role model for you—
so you'd grow up knowing that you wouldn't have to stay
at home or have limited horizons. So you'd know you could
do anything you wanted to, if you tried. Have it all.'

'Did it ever occur to you that it's not possible to have it
all?'

Antonia was silent for a long moment, then shrugged.
'Maybe you're right. So what are you going to do?'

'I think,' Saskia said, 'I'm going to get married.'

Antonia stared at her in shock. 'What? But I thought you
were focused on your career?'

'I was. I still might be. But there's more to life than just
doing my job.' Saskia paused. 'There's someone special in
my life. Someone who's always been there for me, no matter what. He's been very, very patient—and I've kept him
waiting. I just hope I haven't left it too late.'

'You're getting married because you're ill?'

'No. I'm getting married because I love him. It's just
taken me a while to realise it.' Saskia bit her lip. 'That is,
if his offer's still open.'

Antonia suddenly smiled. 'It will be. He wouldn't be
stupid enough to lose you.'

Saskia frowned. 'Meaning?'

'Meaning that you're a very special woman. You're
clever, you're independent and you've got guts.'

'Carry on like this, Mother, and I'll start to think you
might be proud of me,' Saskia said dryly.

'I am. We both are.'

Saskia scoffed. 'You've never been remotely interested in my life.'

'Maybe your father and I are wrapped up a little too much in our jobs,' Antonia admitted. 'But we've always been proud of you. On your graduation day, your father was supposed to be in court. He threw a sickie.'

'He did *what?*' Saskia was truly shocked. Judge Marcus Hayward, QC, would never do such a thing.

'It's not common knowledge. And it's the only time he's ever done it. Well, he probably would have done the day you were born, but men weren't encouraged to be at the birth in those days.' Antonia smiled. 'Don't look so taken aback. We wouldn't have missed your graduation for anything. It was the best day of our lives.'

Saskia couldn't quite believe what she was hearing. 'Even more than when Father took the silk?'

'Even more than that.' Antonia paused. 'Do you have a date for your wedding?'

To make sure it didn't clash with an important case? 'I don't know if there will be one yet. But I'll give you as much advance notice as I can,' Saskia said stiffly.

Antonia waved a hand. 'Oh, it's nothing to do with court schedules, if that's what you're thinking. We're retiring.'

'You're *what?*' She was definitely hearing things now.

'Semi-retiring,' Antonia revised. 'I don't think your father could give up being a judge, and I might become a part-time magistrate. We're taking some time out to travel first. Are you planning to have children?'

'I don't know. It means I'll have to stop taking the anti-rheumatics first, and I'm not sure if that's right for me.'

'Only you can make that decision. And, if you do…maybe I can learn to be a better grandparent than I was a parent.'

Her fastidious mother, in her neat suit—the same kind of clothes, Saskia realised with a twinge of discomfort, that she herself wore to the hospital—no, Antonia couldn't do that. She couldn't sit on the floor and let a baby crawl over her; or sit with a small child who blew raspberries with a mouth full of yoghurt.

Saskia wasn't entirely sure she could do it herself—there was a world of difference between having fun with her godchildren and being able to hand them back before they got tired and grizzly, and being responsible for your own child twenty-four hours a day, seven days a week.

'You'll be fine,' Antonia said. 'You'll learn from my mistakes. You'll still expect a lot from your children, but you'll remember to say the words I always took for granted.' To Saskia's surprise, Antonia put her arms round her and held her close. 'I love you and I'm very, very proud of you. I'm speaking for your father, too.'

Saskia swallowed the huge lump in her throat. 'I never knew.'

'Now you do. And I'm sorry I haven't been there for you when you needed me. I never knew you needed me.'

'I told myself I didn't. That I was independent, like you and Father.'

'You are independent.' Antonia wiped the single tear away with a gentle thumb—the first time Saskia could ever remember her mother mopping her tears. 'And you can have it all, if you want it. RA isn't going to stop you doing anything. All you have to do is let people help you when you need it. That's not being weak. That's being strong—knowing your limitations and dealing with them effectively.'

Saskia remembered her conversation with Connie. *If I had my time over again, it'd be different.* 'Yes.'

'That's my girl.' Antonia finished her coffee and stood up. 'I've got a train to catch. Ring me when you've talked to your man.'

'A train?' Saskia couldn't quite follow.

'Client meeting. I shifted everything from my diary until half past five.'

Antonia had moved things in her diary? For her daughter? 'Supposing I hadn't been here?'

'You were, so don't split hairs.'

Saskia couldn't help laughing as she stood up. 'Considering that's what you do for a living…'

Antonia chuckled. 'Pots and kettles. I know.' Antonia hugged her again, and kissed her on the cheek. 'If you need to talk, I'll be there. A bit late perhaps, and I might not be immediately available, but it's nonetheless heartfelt.'

Saskia nodded. 'Thank you.'

When Antonia had gone, Saskia rang the paediatric ward.

'Hello, is Toby there, please?' she asked when one of the nurses answered.

'Sorry, he's off duty.'

Which meant he was probably at home, Saskia thought.

'I can take a message if you like.'

'Thanks for the offer, but it's OK. I'll call him at home.'

Though this wasn't something she wanted to discuss on the phone. It was face to face or nothing. She grabbed her car keys and drove over to Toby's house. She rang the doorbell, then waited expectantly. Please, don't let her have left it too late.

Except there wasn't any answer.

She considered scribbling him a note, but decided against it. Who knew when he'd get it? For all she knew, he could have decided to spend a few days away from the city, too. Maybe he'd had second thoughts about his offer. Maybe he was out with somebody else right now…

'Oh, stop it. You're being paranoid,' she informed herself, and rang his mobile phone.

She growled in annoyance as she heard the recorded message. His mobile *would* be switched off right when she really needed to talk to him. Why couldn't he have been at work, so she could have met him from his shift? Better still, why couldn't he have been at home, and welcomed her with open arms?

Well, she wasn't going to sit around brooding. She hated not being busy. And there was another important discussion she needed to have. Maybe one she ought to make her priority.

She dialled Jim's direct line.

He answered after the second ring. 'Maternity, Jim Riley speaking.'

'Hi, Jim. It's Saskia. I was wondering...do you have a spare ten minutes or so this afternoon?'

'For you, of course. When?'

'When's a good time?'

'Now?'

'I'm on my way.' She turned off her phone and drove to the hospital.

So this was what it felt like: facing the end of her career. Well, she wasn't used to shrinking from things. The past few months, when she'd realised there was a problem, it had been hell. The indecision, the not knowing. She could have saved herself a lot of heartache if she'd just been brave enough to face facts months ago.

This Christmas would be her first Christmas without delivering a baby. The first Christmas when she didn't have a friendly competition with the midwives and other obstetricians to see who'd have the first Christmas baby and guess the right weight. It was almost unthinkable. But she'd get used to it. She'd cope.

As long as Toby was there.

She forced the flicker of unease to the back of her mind. He'd sounded so sincere the other day. And Toby never said things he didn't mean. He hadn't been trying to let her down gently.

He'd just said that she had to come to him.

Would he believe her? Maybe she should have spoken to Toby first, made sure he knew that she wanted him for himself—not as a substitute for the job she'd given up. If he knew she'd resigned first, maybe he'd think she was just running to him out of panic and didn't really mean it.

Stop it. Not only was she looking at the bridges before she had to cross them, she was lugging the stones and concrete to build them herself, she told herself sharply.

Finally, the moment she dreaded came. She knocked on the door to Jim's office.

He called her in. When she closed the door behind her, he motioned to her to have a seat. 'Ready to talk now?' he asked.

She nodded. 'Jim, I'm sorry to let you down. I'm resigning. I'll give you the official letter tomorrow, but I wanted to tell you myself first.'

'Resigning? But why?' He shook his head. 'You're good at your job—and I thought you were happy here. Or have you been offered a consultant's post somewhere else?'

'I wouldn't have applied for a post without talking to you about it first.' Saskia sighed. 'I love it here, Jim. It's what I was born to do. But I can't do it any more. I've got rheumatoid arthritis. And I just can't put my mums and babies at risk.'

Jim leaned back in his chair and exhaled sharply. 'That was the last thing I expected. How long have you known?'

'Three months. I didn't say anything before, because I didn't want to let you down while you were away. And I thought I could cope.'

'Did you?'

She nodded. 'I managed. But it's getting harder. I thought I might have caused one of our babies to have Erb's palsy, though Toby said it was more likely to be caused by bruising from the birth.'

'Shoulder dystocia?' Jim guessed.

'Yes.'

'Then Toby's probably right.' Jim raised an eyebrow. 'So what are you going to do?'

She shook her head. 'I don't know yet.'

'You don't have to give up being a doctor. You love what you do and you're good at it.'

'But my hands don't always work the way I want them to. I'd be a liability in Theatre, and I can't put my patients at risk.' She sighed. 'There's no other specialty I want to work in. I don't want to be a GP because I like being in the hospital.' She bit her lip. 'I can't see my way out of this right now.'

'Ever thought about teaching?' Jim asked.

Saskia remembered what Connie had said, about how she wished she'd kept her shop because teaching meant you got the pleasure of seeing others develop. The more Saskia thought about it, the more she realised Connie was right: she would enjoy making other people into brilliant doctors and teaching them good bedside manner as well as medicine. Teaching was the perfect compromise.

Then she drooped. 'You know how rare openings are in lecturing. And I want to stay here.' Unless Toby had changed his mind... But she wasn't going to let herself think about that. Not right now.

'I think you'd be good as a lecturer. You've always been good with the students on the ward,' Jim said. 'And I also happen to know there's going to be an opening at the university very shortly. Obviously you'll have to apply, but I can put in a word for you.'

'You'd do that?'

He smiled. 'Of course.'

'So I won't have to give up medicine entirely.'

'Having RA's tough enough. Don't give yourself a hair-shirt to go with it,' he said dryly.

'I've been doing that for the last three months,' she said ruefully. 'I've been an idiot about a lot of things.'

'At least you recognise that now.' He smiled at her. 'So your resignation is accepted, with great regret—and only on condition you ring up the faculty of medicine and get an application form for that teaching job.'

On impulse, Saskia got out of her chair, walked round Jim's side of the desk and gave her boss a hug. 'Thanks, Jim.'

'Any time. Take care—and I'll see you tomorrow.'

'Early shift. Yeah.'

# CHAPTER FIFTEEN

SASKIA tried Toby's mobile again. It was still switched off. Well, fine. That gave her time to sort out something else...a plan that had been growing in her head since she'd left Sussex. And she had a feeling that Toby just might appreciate it.

She found exactly what she wanted in the third jeweller's shop she tried. Better still, they could engrave the message she wanted that very afternoon. She had a coffee and two almond *biscotti* in the café round the corner while she waited for the engraving to be done, then tried Toby's mobile again. Still switched off.

She'd kept him waiting for so long—it really wasn't fair of her to be so impatient now. She just wanted the rest of her life to start this very second... But it looked as if she'd have to wait until tomorrow.

The following morning, she locked her handbag and the all-important box in her locker, then dropped her official resignation letter into Jim's office.

The consultant was already there. 'There was a condition attached,' he reminded her, when he scanned the letter.

'I rang them yesterday afternoon and the application form's in the post.'

'And you'll definitely fill it out?'

She smiled. 'And post it.' If she didn't get the job, she could always try at another university, one a little further away. Manchester, Nottingham, Leicester or Leeds: she had plenty of opportunity. It wasn't the end of the world if she didn't get a post in Sheffield. She'd just have to travel more and compromise a bit.

Compromise. Ha. She must have used that word more times in the last week than she'd used it in her entire life.

The morning sped by. Jim asked her to do the rounds for him while he was in a meeting, and Saskia was pleased to find no complications...until she got to Vanessa Brady in room six. The moment she looked at Vanessa's notes, the words leapt out at her. *Rheumatoid arthritis.* She scanned further down, expecting to see 'nulliparous'— meaning that this was Vanessa's first baby—but was surprised to see that it was her third.

She introduced herself to Vanessa and her husband, Kevin. 'How are you doing?' she asked.

'OK.' Vanessa smiled at her. 'Just can't wait for this little one to arrive. I mean, I usually go into remission when I'm pregnant—'

So she hadn't been diagnosed recently?

'But sulphasalazine doesn't work quite as well for me as methotrexate.'

'How long have you had RA?' Saskia asked.

'Ten years.'

'And this is your third baby?'

'Yes. Everyone said I was crazy, but we wanted another.' She grinned at her husband. 'And it really hasn't made life any harder, has it, love? I mean, I know I had to come off the methotrexate for three months before we started trying, so it didn't affect the baby, but it was worth it. And I was used to taking folic acid anyway, because of the methotrexate.' Patients taking methotrexate were advised to take folic acid, which helped minimise the side effects of the drug. Vanessa laughed. 'Oh, and I waddle more than the average mum.'

'Because your joints are a bit looser.'

'Yeah. But I use hot and cold packs when I can for the

pain, and I go swimming for twenty minutes every other day, and that helps a lot. My rheumatologist told me to avoid ibuprofen and what have you in the third trimester.'

Saskia knew that taking non-steroidal anti-inflammatory drugs, such as ibuprofen, in the last three months of pregnancy could cause heart and liver problems in the baby. 'Are you expecting a flare-up after the birth?' Saskia asked.

Vanessa nodded. 'I usually have quite a bad one, a couple of weeks after the baby's born. And that's why I'm not breast-feeding. I know it's best for baby, but—'

'Your needs are important, too,' Saskia finished. 'If you breast-feed, you can't take the anti-rheumatics because they go into the milk. That means your health's going to suffer, you'll find it harder to cope with the baby, and you'll be struggling when you don't need to.'

'That's what my midwife said, too. And luckily my family's really good—they're always there if we need help, aren't they, love?' Vanessa asked, looking at her husband.

'Better than my lot.' Kevin grimaced. 'They're all panicking that the kids will inherit Nessa's RA.' He rolled his eyes. 'No matter how many articles and books you show them, they're convinced they know best.'

'I know the type,' Saskia said feelingly. She couldn't help asking, 'Do you find you need a lot of help?'

'If I get a bad flare-up, it's difficult to change a nappy or do up the poppers on a sleepsuit,' Vanessa admitted. 'So I've learned to be sensible about pacing myself. If the house looks a tip, I don't stress about it as much as I used to: I just get the kids to chuck everything into one of those big pop-up tidy bags. And somebody else is doing all the Christmas dinner and stuff this year, not me.'

'Sounds like a good plan.' Saskia examined Vanessa and checked her blood pressure, then checked the baby's heartbeat. 'Everything looks absolutely fine.'

'Yeah. Kev's well trained on the TENS machine now.'

Vanessa smiled. 'That and a back rub should get me through to delivery.'

Saskia could imagine Toby doing the same. He'd be with her every step of the way, making sure she didn't overdo things and caring for her.

Hell. It was the first time she'd ever even thought about becoming pregnant. In all the years she'd worked on the maternity unit, she'd never imagined herself there, in the early stages of labour, waiting for her baby to arrive. And now here she was, with a vision of herself carrying Toby's baby.

'Are you all right?' Kevin asked.

Obviously the shock must have shown in her face. She forced herself to smile. 'I'm fine, thanks. It's just...I was diagnosed with rheumatoid arthritis myself three months ago.'

'It's scary,' Vanessa said. 'The hardest thing is accepting that you've got it—getting over the "why me?" bit. Once you've done that, it gets easier.' She smiled at Saskia. 'What are you on?'

'Methotrexate—weekly tablet.' She hadn't been able to face the idea of a weekly intramuscular injection. 'It's not having much effect yet.'

'Give it another couple of months. You'll feel better then,' Vanessa reassured her.

Saskia smiled wryly. 'Listen to us. I'm supposed to be the one reassuring you.'

'No problem. If you want a chat about it, you know where I am,' Vanessa said. 'I'm not going very far for the next couple of days.'

'Thanks. I might just do that,' Saskia said.

She left the room, her mind whirling. Vanessa was having her third baby. It *was* possible to have children and have RA and still cope with everything. So maybe Antonia was right after all, and she could have it all. A job she loved, a man she loved and a family.

And she couldn't wait for them any longer.

She rang down to Paediatrics. To her delight, Judy, Toby's registrar, answered the phone.

'Hi, Judy, it's Saskia. Is Toby in today?'

'Yes. Do you want me to put you through to him?'

'No. But can you do me a huge favour, please? Get him into his office and keep him there for me. Lie to him, do anything you have to, but keep him in his office.'

Judy sounded suspicious. 'What's going on?'

'I can't say right now—but I promise you'll be the first to know.'

'Saskia, be gentle with him. He's a really nice bloke.'

'I know. And I'm...' Saskia's voice caught. Did other people really think she would hurt Toby? Or had she already hurt him badly, and she was the only one not to have noticed? 'Please, Judy. I wouldn't ask if it wasn't important. And, whatever you might think, Toby's important to me.' More than important. But she wanted to tell *him* that first.

'OK. I'm just saying he's been down for the last few days. It's not like him. And we haven't seen you around recently either.'

'I've been away.' Guilt flickered in her stomach. 'I'm on my way down.' She hung up, told Georgina she was on a break, collected the box from her locker and shoved it in the pocket of her white coat, then headed for the paediatric ward.

'He's in his office,' Judy said, when she saw Saskia.

'Thank you. I owe you,' Saskia said softly. 'And, I promise you, I'd never hurt Toby.'

She rapped on Toby's office door. There was tinsel taped all the way round it, and his door was virtually covered in home-made Christmas cards from his tiny patients. Saskia had been feeling more like Scrooge over the last couple of weeks, all 'bah, humbug'. Now, she found herself humming 'We Wish You a Merry Christmas.' And, if this worked out…it would be more than a happy new year.

'Come in,' Toby called.

She closed the door behind her, locked it and pulled the blinds.

Toby frowned. 'Why are you doing that?'

'Because.'

He wasn't smiling, she noticed. Didn't look pleased to see her. Fear lurched in her stomach. Had she left it too late?

'I didn't know you were back,' he said.

'I came back yesterday.'

He folded his arms. 'You didn't ring.'

'Yes, I did.' She walked over to his desk and sat on the edge. 'You were off duty, you weren't at home and your mobile was switched off all evening.'

'Because I was out with the team, ten-pin bowling. It was our Christmas meal.'

And she'd forgotten. She'd felt so un-Christmassy, she'd even agreed to cover the department instead of going out for their Christmas meal.

'I didn't bother keeping my mobile phone on—I didn't think I'd be able to hear it over all the noise at the bowling alley. And you didn't leave a message.'

'I wanted to talk to you face to face, not on the phone. Did you win?'

'Yeah. How did you get on with Connie?'

Saskia nodded. 'OK. I understand her more now.'

'And?'

'I resigned this morning.'

He looked at her, unsmiling. 'What are you going to do?'

'Teach medicine, among other things. If I get the job,

that is.' She smiled. 'I'm applying for a lecturer's position at the university. Jim's going to put in a word for me.'

Toby's face was unreadable. 'What other things?'

'Ah, yes.' This could be the biggest mistake she'd ever made in her life. Or it could be the moment the sun came back into her world for good. It was a risk. A risk she had to take. She fished in her pocket and handed him the box.

'What's this?'

'Early Christmas present.'

A muscle flickered in his jaw. 'It's still three weeks until Christmas.'

'That's OK. You can open it now.'

'I never open presents early.'

No way could she wait another three weeks. 'Toby—just open it, will you? Please?'

He unwrapped it. Painfully slowly. She wanted to scream. Why couldn't he just rip the paper off, as she would have done?

Then he opened the box and whistled as he saw the designer watch. 'This must have cost you a fortune! It's too much.'

'No.' She shook her head. It wasn't nearly enough. 'I wanted to buy it for you. I thought you'd like it.'

'I do. It's beautiful.'

'Um, it's engraved.'

He took the watch out of the box, turned it over and read the message engraved on the back. *Toby. I love you. For ever. Saskia.*

Still, he was silent. And his face was unreadable.

Oh, God.

She *had* left it too late.

'I'm sorry. Look, just forget I...' She slid off his desk and backed away. Five seconds and she'd be at the door. Half a minute to walk off the ward. And then she could run.

'Do you mean this?' His voice cut through her panic.

She looked at him, and he was reading the card she'd left inside the box. A tiny, tiny card. She'd written just four words inside it. *Will you marry me?*

She walked backwards until her back leaned against his door. 'You said I had to come to you,' she whispered.

'Mmm-hmm.'

Oh, God, how much longer was he going to make her wait? How much longer was he going to torture her like this?

She'd made a fool of herself. A colossal fool. She fumbled behind her for the lock, knowing that she had to get out of there. Right now.

'Say it.' His voice was hoarse, and her gaze snapped back to his face. When she saw the tortured look in his eyes, her hands dropped to her sides again.

She owed him this.

At the very least.

'I love you, Toby.'

He was silent. As if he didn't believe what he was hearing. She could hardly blame him. She'd pushed him away for so long, he probably thought that he was having auditory hallucinations. 'I love you,' she repeated. 'It's taken me long enough to realise it. But you were right. None of my men lasted more than two dates because they weren't you. And I was running from the idea of being with you for the rest of my life, because I was scared. I was scared I couldn't give you what you wanted, what you deserved.'

'So what's changed your mind?'

'I talked to Connie. She was engaged. But she broke it off when she was diagnosed with RA, because she was scared she'd be a burden—ironically, the burden she actually became. But if she'd given Hugh the choice, he would have chosen her. The whole circle would never have started—being lonely, demanding attention and wanting more whenever she got it, which pushed people away, which made her feel lonelier and demand more attention.' Saskia's shoulders drooped. 'That's what I could become.'

'And you think that marrying me would stop that happening to you.'

It was a statement, not a question. He obviously felt used. Which wasn't what she'd intended at all. 'No. It's not that. While I was away, I thought about you, Toby. You're the first person I talk to when anything happens, good or bad. You're the first person I think of when I wake up in the morning. You're the last person I think of at night before I fall asleep. And I've been very, very stupid. Selfish. I've taken you for granted—and I won't do that again.' She swallowed hard. 'One of my mums this morning…she has RA. This is her third child. She's taking—well, *was* taking,' she amended, 'the same medication as me. I just have to stop it for three months before we try for a baby.'

His eyes widened. 'Are you telling me you want a baby?'

'For the first time in my life, today, I imagined myself on the ward instead of one of my mums. In labour.' Her lips twitched. 'I never thought I'd be broody. Or that it would happen just like that—one minute I'd be my normal self, and the next I'd… No.' She shook her head. 'I don't want *a* baby. I want *your* baby, Toby. I want to make love with you. I want to make a life with you. I want to feel our child kicking inside me.'

He folded his arms. 'So, let me get this straight. You've resigned, you want a baby and you've decided to marry me.'

'No. I've resigned. I've applied for a job I can do without putting anyone at risk—a job I think would be right for me, and would fit around our kids if we're lucky enough to have them. And I've realised something I think I've known, deep inside, for a very long time: that you're the one I want to spend the rest of my life with.' She took a deep breath.

'I told you if I ever got married, it would be to someone I liked, trusted and respected.'

'So you like, trust and respect me.'

She nodded. 'There was something missing from my list. Love.' She lifted her chin. 'I love you, Toby. I've loved you for years, but I was in denial. I'm not in denial any more, not about anything. I love you, and I want to spend the rest of my life with you.' She spread her hands. 'Though I can't promise you perfection.'

'And, as I once told you, I don't want perfection. I want you.'

'So is that a yes, then?'

It took him two seconds to get from his desk to the door. The moment his mouth came down on hers, Saskia completely lost track of time. But when he broke the kiss and smiled, she knew his answer.

Yes.

# EPILOGUE

*Three years later*

BREAKFAST in bed?' Toby sat up and kissed his wife. 'Angel.' Then he frowned. 'Hang on, it's my turn to be house-husband today.'

'And?' Saskia asked.

'So I should have brought *you* breakfast in bed before you go to work.'

She shook her head, smiling. 'You deserve it. You were up half the night with Connie.' Their eighteen-month-old daughter had woken in the night, crying, and Toby had left Saskia to sleep and had settled the baby himself.

'What's this?' He picked up the neatly wrapped package on the side of the tray.

'Early Christmas present.'

He groaned. 'The last early Christmas present you gave me pole-axed me.'

This one would, too. She hugged herself with delight and sat on the side of the bed. 'Just open it, will you? Or I'll be late for my class.'

Toby laughed. 'I suppose your students will stop being scared of you if you're late in—they'll realise you're not absolutely perfect, so they won't panic about making sure they're on time for your lectures in future.'

She pulled a face at him. 'My students are *not* scared of me.'

He scoffed. 'They are! I've heard them whispering in the hospital. When they find out I'm married to you, they start tiptoeing around me as well.'

'Oh, ha, ha.' She bounced on the bed. 'Open it, Tobe.'

'Nearly three years of marriage, and my legendary patience still hasn't rubbed off on you.' He tutted, but unwrapped the parcel. Then his eyes widened as he realised what it was. A pregnancy test. 'Two blue lines?' he breathed.

'Positive,' she confirmed with a grin. 'Happy Christmas, Mr Barker. You're going to be a daddy. Again.'

Ignoring the breakfast tray, he flung his arms round her and kissed her. 'Happy Christmas, Dr Hayward. Even though you're a liar.'

'Liar?' She frowned. 'How so?'

'You said you couldn't give me perfection. Look at us now. Me a part-time consultant and a part-time househusband, you a part-time lecturer and a part-time slave to our daughter. I get to have lunch with the two women I love most in the world at least twice a week. And...' He stroked her stomach. 'It just gets better and better.'

'Toby, if something gets better, then it's not perfect in the first place,' she pointed out.

He laughed. 'Oh, light of my life, has anyone told you how easy it is to tell that your parents are lawyers?'

She hit him with a pillow. 'Drink your coffee and get up, or you'll be late for toddler group this morning.'

'Don't care. It's still perfection.' He grinned. 'And it's getting better every day.'

'You know, my mother was right in the end. It is possible to have it all,' she said softly. 'The man I love, the family I love and the job I love.' Even her parents seemed different now: much closer to her since their retirement, than they had been, and they were both besotted grandparents. Toby's parents had welcomed her, and Connie had become the chair of the Horticultural Society and was busy trying to breed an azalea to name after her great-niece and namesake.

'All you had to do was learn to compromise,' Toby said.

'No.' She kissed him. 'All I had to do was realise how much I love you. Now, and for the rest of our days.'

# DON'T MISS...

the books in this mini-series:

## 24/7

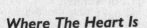

**Where The Heart Is**
Kate Hardy
September 2005

**The Heroic Surgeon**
Olivia Gates
November 2005

**The Consultant's Christmas Proposal**
Kate Hardy
December 2005

**The Surgeon's Rescue Mission**
Dianne Drake
February 2006

**The Doctor's Courageous Bride**
Dianne Drake
March 2006

### AVAILABLE FROM

Target • K-Mart • Big W
• selected supermarkets
• bookstores • newsagents

**OR**

Call Harlequin Mills & Boon
on 1300 659 500 to order now
for the cost of a local call.
NZ customers call (09) 837 1553.

**Shop on-line at www.eHarlequin.com.au**

Books only available from Harlequin Mills & Boon
for 3 months after the publishing date.
Release dates may be subject to change.

# Available Next Month

**Prescription: Marry Her Immediately**
Jacqueline Diamond

**A Child To Call Her Own**
Gill Sanderson

**Gift Of A Family**
Sarah Morgan

**The Life Saver**
Lilian Darcy

**A Surgeon Worth Waiting For**
Melanie Milburne

**The Noble Doctor**
Gill Sanderson

## AVAILABLE FROM

Target • K-Mart • Big W • Borders • selected supermarkets
• bookstores • newsagents

OR

Call Harlequin Mills & Boon on 1300 659 500 to order
for the cost of a local call. NZ customers call (09) 837 1553.

**Shop on-line at www.eHarlequin.com.au**

6 Brand New Stories Each Month

Harlequin
Mills & Boon

medical

*on-the-pulse*

*medical*

*dramas*

# THE FORTUNES OF TEXAS: Reunion

**THE PRICE OF PRIVILEGE. THE POWER OF FAMILY.**

**The Fortunes of Texas are back with a long-awaited new 12 book collection!**

Featuring all of your favourite authors including Ann Major, Marie Ferrarella and Laurie Paige.

**TWO BOOKS EACH MONTH**

## BEGINS JANUARY 2006

AVAILABLE FROM BIG W, KMART, TARGET, BORDERS NEWSAGENCIES AND SELECTED BOOKSTORES.

Shop online at www.eHarlequin.com.au
or call 1300 659 500 (AU), 09 837 1553 (NZ) for home delivery

FT1205

# NORA ROBERTS

## THE MacKADE BROTHERS

*The sinfully sexy MacKade brothers are back!*

## DON'T MISS OUT ON THIS BEAUTIFUL FOUR BOOK COLLECTION.

## BEGINS JANUARY 2006

AVAILABLE FROM BIG W, KMART, TARGET, BORDERS
NEWSAGENCIES AND SELECTED BOOKSTORES.

Shop online at www.eHarlequin.com.au
or call 1300 659 500 (AU), 09 837 1553 (NZ) for home delivery

MB1205

# Get your favourite books
## delivered direct to your home!

There's so many benefits - here's why you should subscribe:

☑ **FREE Home Delivery** - no postage and handling charge.

☑ **No risk and no obligation** - no minimum number of books you have to buy and you can cancel or suspend your subscription at anytime!

☑ **Get your books earlier than the stores** - delivered direct to your home!

☑ **Our friendly customer service team really do care** - they are more than happy to answer any questions and help with your account.

☑ **You'll never need to search in the bookstores again** - the best books will be delivered to your home every month.

☑ **Choose from 13 different series of romance novels** - there really is something for everyone!

# Call now!
## Australia: 1300 659 500
## New Zealand: (09) 837 1553

DTC01

# Send in for a
# FREE BOOK
## today!

How would you like to escape into a world of romance and excitement? A world in which you can experience all the glamour and allure of romance and seduction?

## No purchase necessary - now or ever!

To receive your FREE Harlequin Mills & Boon romance novel, simply fill in the coupon and send it to the address below, together with $1.00 worth of loose postage stamps (80 cents in NZ) to cover postage and handling (please do not send money orders or cheques). There is never an obligation to buy!

**Send to: HARLEQUIN MILLS & BOON FREE BOOK OFFER**
**Aust: PO Box 693, Sawberry Hills, NSW, 2012**
**NZ: Private Bag 92122, Auckland, 1020**

*Harlequin Mills ❤ Boon*
*Direct to you*

✂ ─ ─ ─ ─ ─ ─ ─ ─ ─ ─ ─ ─ ─ ─ ─ ─ ─ ─ ─

Please send me my FREE Harlequin Mills & Boon Sexy romance valued at $6.15 (NZ$7.25). I have included $1.00 worth of loose postage stamps (80 cents NZ). Please do not stick them to anything.

Name: Mrs / Ms / Miss / _____

Address: _____

_____ P/Code _____

Daytime Tel. No.: (\_\_\_\_) _____

FBBP05/Z F BBP5

This offer is restricted to one free book per household. Only original coupons with $1.00 worth of loose postage stamps (80 cents in NZ) will be accepted. Your book may differ from those shown. Expires 31st December, 2005 or while stocks last. Offer only available to Aust and NZ residents over 18 years. You may also receive offers from other reliable companies as a result of this application. If you do not wish to share in this opportunity please tick the box. □